BRIMSTONE AND BROOMSTICKS

ACCIDENTAL WITCHES BOOK 1

DEBRA DUNBAR

CHAPTER 1

LUCIEN

"*H*ere? Seriously?"

I stared at the dilapidated building, at the flickering neon sign announcing the joint to be Pistol Pete's, at the enormous oil stain in the parking space next to what I took to be the front door. When I'd told Charon to take me "anywhere", I'd expected a swank club or a political fundraiser, or the middle of a gruesome battle, not a dime-beer bar in some rinky-dink town called Accident.

"Don't judge a drinking establishment by its paint-peeled siding," he told me.

I was totally judging this establishment. And the town. And by association all the residents. The only reason I wasn't throttling Charon right now was because there'd been a strange zing of electricity we'd passed through about a mile down the road that had piqued my curiosity. Ley lines? Remnants from some arcane ritual? An old crossroad summoning?

"I'm trusting you on this one, Charon," I warned.

The demon grinned. "Have fun. Call me when you're ready to return to hell."

I fingered the coin in my pocket and nodded, assuming this was probably payback for something I'd done centuries ago. No one held a grudge like Charon. And no one would dare to stick it to me like this besides Charon either. Outside of being summoned or granted what amounted to a travel visa, he was my only ticket out of hell.

And my only ticket back to hell.

Charon laughed, the sound very much like nails on a chalkboard, then vanished, leaving me to either find something to entertain myself in this…Pistol Pete's, or walk down what looked like a long road and hope to come across an orgy, or at the very least someone screwing a goat.

I wasn't into people screwing goats. Sacrificing a goat: yes. Screwing one: no. The entertainment in the latter would be the punishment of said individuals, not because of any sort of interest in the carnal act they were performing.

Punishment. That was the mission statement for hell's minions and I embraced my job with all the wholehearted enjoyment of a spawn of Satan, because, well, I *was* a spawn of Satan. Technically this was a vacation, but when something was pretty much your entire reason for existence, was there ever *really* a vacation?

I headed through the parking lot and saw a group of women walking out the door of the bar—tiny, well-proportioned women with tight clothing and fuck-me stilettos.

Their skin was an odd pearlescent gray color. They had glittery, translucent wings and pointed ears that rose like pale, thin horns through the fine curtain of their identically shaded platinum blonde hair. They laughed, and it sounded like a high-pitched silver-bells sound that humans never have, no matter how much they like to describe female laughter as such.

I stopped in the parking lot and gawked. I'd seen fairies before, but not strolling out of a bar without any attempt at glamour to mask their non-human appearance. One of them saw me and flashed me a row of jagged teeth in her red slash of a mouth.

"Look girls, it's a newbie!"

They strolled over towards me. If I'd been human, I would have been fighting the urge to flee, but instead I was intrigued. And entertained. Huh. Charon was right. This might be a fun evening after all.

"Let's take him home," one purred before giving me a toothy smile. "We won't bite. Much."

"Careful," one of her friends warned. "We have to follow the rules."

"Bah, rules," her companion scoffed. "Those witches haven't done anything to enforce the rules since the old lady died. We can do what we want. This newbie vanishes, and no one will know."

"Or care," one of the others added. "That stupid dryad of a sheriff can't figure out his ass from a hole in the wall. And the witches don't care."

Normally I would have been all up for fairy orgy action, especially since they would have gotten the surprise of their dramatically shortened lives once they tried to kill me. But there was one word that pushed every thought of a fairy massacre out of my mind.

"Witch?" I stuttered, suddenly a bumbling fool instead of a powerful demon. We demons respected witches. In a disagreement, they were fully capable of opening a whole can of whoop-ass on us. But our relationship over the many millennia had rarely been contentious. Witch energy was like a drug—sensual and captivating. Getting summoned by a coven, becoming their go-to demon was the dream of every one of hell's minions. Partnering with a witch meant the perfect power combo. We were stronger with them. They were stronger with us. Yes, there were some trade-offs on either side, but overall it was a win-win situation.

The only problem was that roughly two thousand years ago the humans had decided to kill off the witches. There were a few internet frauds and weak wannabes, but we demons hadn't seen a real witch in a toad's age. Was there really a witch in this town? Witches? Or were these fairies just blowing smoke up my ass?

One of the women sidled up next to me. "Don't you worry about witches, sweetheart. They can't even start a fire without a match and a gallon of gasoline. Unless they're in the courthouse with their ex-boyfriend that is."

The whole group erupted into their wind-chime laughter, leaving me wondering about the joke I'd obviously not gotten. So *not* real witches, then. Damn. I'd hoped otherwise, but just because these fairies were bold enough to walk around without glamour didn't mean there were actual witches nearby.

"Leave him alone girls," a voice behind me rumbled. "Go find some pixies to torment."

An arm came around my shoulder and I turned to see myself facing a satyr.

"Come on," the satyr told me. "I'll buy you a drink."

The only coin I had was the one I needed to call Charon, so I let the satyr lead me into the bar, the fairies behind me promising all sorts of naughty fun later if I was interested and still alive.

Fairies. A man with spiraled horns rising from his curly dark hair, the lower half of him furred and cloven-hooved with a twitchy tail and oddly angled legs. Let's just say it prepared me for what I saw when I walked through the door of the bar.

There were maybe a dozen humans in there. Nine of them had glowing gold eyes that made me immediately realize they weren't actually humans. The rest of the population had fur or scales, or snakes for hair. There were cockatrices, elves, ogres, and even a smallish dragon wedged over near the band, apparently assisting with pyrotechnics. The silence outside that had made the dive bar seem vacant had magically vanished the moment my satyr friend opened the door. The music pounded. Voices, grunts, growls, and squeals merged in a cacophony of sound.

"Here." My satyr friend pushed a drink into my hand, then clinked his glass against mine. "Bottom's up."

I threw down the liquor, realizing the moment it hit my stomach that it was far stronger than most human alcoholic beverages.

"I'm Jeff." He slapped the glass on the bar and stuck out his hand. "A satyr, obviously."

"Lucien." I shook his hand, admiring the man's grip. "I'm a demon."

He nodded. "I figured as much. You not freaking out about the girls in the parking lot, not batting an eyelid over my appearance, and the fact that you just threw down a shot of dragon's bane and didn't fall to the floor in convulsions clued me in. A word to the wise, my friend? Ditch the human form or everyone is going to think you're a newbie and pester the heck out of you."

I hadn't revealed my demon form outside of hell in three thousand years, and I wasn't about to do it now, even surrounded by all these other non-human beings.

The satyr shrugged. "Suit yourself, bro. There's a nymph over there giving me the eye, so you're on your own. The ogres are assholes. Fairies bite. Don't mess with the dragon unless you don't mind a few burns. Oh, and avoid the shifters —especially the werewolves. It's two nights before the full moon, so they're all itching to fight and fuck, and they're not particular about which of those they're doing."

"Those folk with the glowing eyes?" I nodded toward the four men and two women at the end of the bar.

"Yep. Good luck. And don't kill anyone. Those fairies might not think our sheriff is all that, but he's got back-up if you know what I mean."

I didn't, but I nodded anyway. This was the first time in nearly three thousand years that I felt astonished, surprised, ready to go with the flow and enjoy whatever hand fate dealt me. And when I got back to hell, Charon was getting a serious bonus. This place rocked.

Jeff wandered off toward the beckoning nymph. I ordered a drink and put it on my "tab", then walked right over to the group of shifters. Hey, it was my vacation. Might as well make the most of it and possibly combine business with pleasure.

Three drinks and fifteen minutes later I was back in the parking lot, trying to beat the shit out of a werewolf. The drink was hitting me harder than it should have. The werewolf was hitting me harder than he should have. I was beginning to feel less like a demon and more like the newbie/human they'd accused me of being.

Forget the ogres being assholes, these werewolves definitely were. Well, four of them were. The other two were interested bystanders to the whole thing. One of the onlookers, a female with the sort of curves that made a demon salivate, seemed particularly fascinated by the fight. Maybe if I played my cards right…

But I couldn't really pay much attention to her, because for the first time in my life, I needed to focus on my opponent. A werewolf. An interesting challenge, but if someone had told me I'd be struggling to keep from getting pummeled by a damned werewolf, I would have laughed.

The guy hit me. Hard. I saw a flash of light and staggered to the side, throwing my arms up to ward off a second blow.

I shook my head, but the pain didn't go away. My face throbbed where he'd punched me, and something wet tickled at the edge of my lip. I licked it and tasted copper. Blood. I knew what blood tasted like, but I wasn't used to tasting my own.

Why wasn't I healing? And more importantly, why was I so slow? Why was I unable to lay this werewolf onto the asphalt with one blow? Why was this so…difficult?

The guy hit me again, this time in the midsection, causing me to double over in pain. Okay. Enough of this shit. I couldn't recall a time when I'd ever been on the losing side of a fight. My left hook usually knocked an opponent out, but this guy wasn't going down no matter how many times I hammered him.

Another blow sent my head to the side. I felt blood trickle down my cheek and squinted to focus. Screw it. Pulling my power from deep inside, I went to incinerate this asshole where he stood. Nothing happened. Well, nothing except two more blows into my stomach that sent me to my knees.

The crowd cheered. Rage flooded me. My abilities might be somehow blunted, but I was still a demon. There was no way in hell I was going to let a damned werewolf get the upper hand here. With a roar I got to my feet and let my anger take the wheel.

The werewolf went down, but I hadn't banked on his buddies finally deciding to back him up. By the time I heard the sirens pulling into the parking lot, I was fighting four werewolves instead of one—and losing.

A law enforcement individual got out of his car, holding what appeared to be a stick in his hand. I ignored his shouted commands to break it up, figuring that stick couldn't do anything this asshole's fists hadn't already done. One of my assailants stepped back with hands raised. The others kept fighting—me as well.

"Break. It. Up." He waved the stick. "Let him alone, Clinton. "Killing the newbs is bad for tourism."

"We don't need no fuckin' tourism." The werewolf snarled from his position on the ground while I danced around, landing the occasional blow on his three remaining defenders—and taking far more blows than I was landing. The curvy wolf on the sidelines began to chant for Clinton to get up and fight.

"Back. Down." The guy with the badge and the stick slapped it against the side of his leg.

Was this the sheriff? The fairies had said the sheriff was a dryad, but in my experience tree nymphs were always female. So if this guy was the dryad sheriff, he was a Drus, and part of the Mediterranean nymph families instead of the Celtic ones I was more familiar with.

One of the werewolves pulled a knife and I reacted, twisting his arm until it snapped. He dropped the knife, but not before I felt the sting of three rapid slices across my chest and side.

The dude with the badge swung the stick and shouted a word. It sparked and blue fireworks hit us all, knocking everyone except the two bystanders to the ground.

Clinton groaned, then cursed, then threw up on the ground and began to shake. The wolf with the broken arm began to cry, cradling the limb. One of the downed wolves staggered to his feet and ran, or rather limped, toward the wooded section at the end of the parking lot. The other stayed down, staring up at the Law with wide eyes and raised hands.

"Who are you?" The cop glared at me instead of the three remaining werewolves who'd attacked me.

Okay, maybe I *had* started the whole thing, but I sure as hell hadn't banked on having this guy's buddies join in, or somehow being blunted of my infernal powers in this weird town.

"Who. Are. You?" The Law slapped the bully stick against his palm and I eyed it, knowing instinctively that I didn't want to get hit with that thing.

"Lucien." I spat some blood onto the pavement, happy that some splattered the Law's shoes.

"Stranger in town, Lucien?" He smacked the stick once more against his palm. Why wasn't he providing medical attention to the moaning werewolves? Or arresting them? They'd…well, sort of ganged up on me.

"Humans gotta be careful here, Lucien," the Law commented. "Maybe not provoke werewolves two nights before the full moon. Maybe apologize and walk away rather than try to take on four shifters in a parking lot. You got a death wish, buddy?"

He thought I was human. How cute. Jeff-the-satyr's words came back to me and I grinned. "Just taking out the trash, officer. You gonna arrest these guys for disturbing the peace?"

"No." The man pulled a pair of handcuffs from his utility belt. I felt them. I felt that there was more to these things than metal, and instinctively recoiled.

"I'm filing charges," Clinton whined. "He attacked me. Look at me. Assault. Look at Stanley. Lock him up. He's a threat to everyone in this town."

"What are you, Lucien?" The Law looked at Clinton and Stanley, at the terrified werewolf with his hands raised, then he sent a narrowed glance my way. "What are you?"

"A human," I lied. It felt cowardly to do so, but I really didn't want him to put those weird handcuffs on me.

He bent down and reached for my arm. I dug in my pocket for the coin. *Now would be a good time, Charon.*

Nothing happened. The Law yanked my hand out of my pocket and clapped the handcuffs on me.

Suddenly I felt as if I was in a fishbowl, unable to escape. I had no idea what was happening, but I had none of my infernal powers, and the coin that was supposed to summon my ride wasn't working.

Accident. Whatever town this was, me being here was no accident. And when I found Charon, that cursed traitor, he was going to die. Die permanently.

CHAPTER 2

CASSANDRA

"Got a case for you, Cass." Mack sat on the edge of my desk, chewing on a toothpick with the vigor of a lumberjack cutting down old growth pine. "Assault two. Two counts. Possible drunk and disorderly."

I stared at the inbox stack of folders that precariously teetered two feet above my desk, then over at the six boxes lined up in mini-towers against the wall.

"Give it to Russ. It's his turn." I had six DWIs, two protective orders, and a burglary. Besides, I had more seniority than Russ. The partners should be dumping the crap cases on him, not me.

"He's claiming to be the son of the devil."

"Then call a psychiatrist as well as sending Russ over. It's not my turn." Where was the Mossburg file? That last deposition? It was here on my desk somewhere.

"It's in Accident. City limits."

I hesitated, knowing full well what happened inside Accident city limits. Nope. Not my problem. Even though I lived there, not my problem. Even though over three hundred years of my family had lived there, even though my ancestor had founded the town, still not my problem.

"Send Russ."

Mack gnawed the toothpick. "It's your turn, Cass. And if he's really the son of Satan…"

"Are you joking? Lucifer Junior wouldn't be cooling his heels in a jail cell waiting for whoever was on rotation for pro-bono work. He'd vanish in a puff of smoke and… I don't know, be burning a church down in Georgia or something."

Mack snickered. "You got wards in Accident. He's probably a bit surprised and pissed about that right now, since last time I checked y'all didn't count demons among your town residents."

We didn't. And the only reason Mack knew about Accident and the wards was because the partners of the law firm were sphinx and Mack was a wulver. None of them resided within Accident city limits, but they liked to live, and work, a quick dash away from the town, just in case.

Not that any of this was my business. Of course, if my bosses thought otherwise…

"I'm busy. Send Russ."

Mack scowled. "Partners say he's a demon, so he's your problem."

I scowled back. "Well if he's a demon, then he picked the wrong town for a vacation from hell, didn't he?" Speaking of hell, where *was* that Mossburg file? "Actually, I doubt the wards are strong enough to cut the balls off the son of Satan. They're not as effective on demons as I wished they were. He's a human, a newb. He's not a demon, and it's not my case."

"Son of Satan, Cass. You're the witch in this law firm. You're supposed to take care of the rogue supes, even if you've decided that you don't give a shit about Accident and what happens there."

That was so unfair. Kinda true, but still unfair.

"He's not the son of Satan and it's not my turn. Send a psychiatrist, or a priest." I spotted a file peeking out from under Mack's leg. "And get up. You're sitting on the Mossburg deposition."

"Rogue supe. He offered the warden one wish if he set him free."

"I hope the warden took him up on that." I tugged on the file, but two hundred pounds of man-butt held it in place.

"Cass." There was a tired pleading note in Mack's voice that finally got my attention. And his earlier comment had stung. I *did* care about Accident. I just wasn't about to become the witch-in-charge. I wanted to be a resident, to live my life without all the heap of responsibility that others wanted to dump on my shoulders.

Including this stupid case. But if the partners, sphinx or not, decided I needed to handle it, then I better get my ass in gear.

"If this is just another whack-job, I'm going to be pissed," I warned him.

"Here's the info. He's in county lockup." Mack got up to leave, finally freeing the Mossburg file. "Oh, and make sure you take your pointed hat. Just in case he tries to drag you off to hell or something."

"I don't have a pointed hat!" I shouted after his retreating back.

There was a reason I got these cases and it didn't have anything to do with gender inequality in the law firm. Well, sometimes it didn't have to do with gender inequality in the law firm. Since I'd gotten my job here they'd been using my particular gifts as an excuse for dumping all sorts of unsavory cases on my desk. That protective order hadn't been because some woman was *really* cursing her boyfriend. The one DWI guy didn't *really* cast an illusion spell at the scene of an accident. And last month's poisoning had just been a normal poisoning, not a potion brewed in a cauldron under a full moon. Sometimes it was a pain being one of the descendants of the greatest witch in the last three hundred years who'd also been one of the few women to escape the Salem Witch Trials. It was my ancestor who'd founded Accident and cast the wards that made it a haven for persecuted supernaturals. Sometimes it was a pain living in one of the few towns where the presence of supernatural creatures and magic was a given.

But that was why my great, great, great, great, great (five greats) grandmother Temperance Perkins had founded this town. No excommunication. No burning at the stake. Over the centuries Accident had become a town full of werewolves and vampires and harpies and fairies, and most importantly, a town that wouldn't cast stones at witches practicing the not-so-dark arts.

Before I headed off to the town detention center, I opened the file and uttered a soft 'whoa' at the mug shot. Hot damn. Even with some fresh bruises that had no doubt gotten even more colorful after a night in jail, the guy was smoking. Not that I particularly wanted to get naked with a D and D/assault two, but…damn. Hot damn.

Tearing my eyes from the picture, I scanned the arrest notes. Huh. Looked like he'd had the upper hand with Clinton Dickskin before a few of Clinton's buddies stepped in to help out. That wasn't easy to do given that Clinton was one of the town's more beefy and belligerent werewolves and wasn't known for holding back on his punches. Even with four against one, Hottie McHotpants had made an impressive showing before the sheriff got there and magic-bombed the whole lot of them. Out of the four, one had gone to the hospital for stitches and a compound fracture, one probably should have gone to the hospital for stitches but refused treatment, and Clinton had gone downtown to press charges —which made me wonder about the human who was handy enough with his fists to make one of the baddest werewolves in town cry assault.

It wasn't the first time Clinton Dickskin had gotten into a fight. Probably wouldn't be the last time, although I can't recall him ever getting the crap beat out of him to the point that he whined to the law. Who the hell was this guy, Chuck Norris? Whoever he was, half the town would want to buy him a beer once this was over. If he stayed in town, that was.

Back to my client, Infernal Hottie. Oh no. I stood corrected, he actually had a name according to the police report, although no ID and, of course, no money. Lucien. No last name. He told the cop he didn't need a last name because he was the son of Lucifer. Great. I rolled my eyes. Figures I'd get the whack-job. I was probably going to have to call in psych after all.

I read on.

No ID. Bit of a dust up with Clinton in Pistol Pete's around midnight according to the bartender. Bouncer threw the werewolf out. Clinton's buddies protested, so Lucifer got shown the door as well, just to keep peace and be fair and all. Someone called in the fight in the parking lot. When the sheriff arrived, he found Clinton looking like he'd been driven over by a 1998 Jeep Grand Cherokee. Human arrested. Bus called in for two werewolves. Paramedics found one with bruises and cuts, another with a rather interesting compound fracture as well as cuts and bruises. The human had cuts and bruises. Clinton had cuts and bruises, including a rather deep one on the head from being shoved head-first rather forcefully into the window of a nearby truck. All except for the wolf with the broken arm refused transport, and Clinton insisted that charges be pressed.

Hellboy, on the other hand, seemed surprisingly

unharmed for having been in a fight with four werewolves. There were a few claw wounds about two inches long on his forearm, side, and chest, judged by the paramedics as not deep enough to require stitches. Hellboy had refused medical treatment as well.

Huh. The guy was a smoking specimen of male physique and he fought like some ninja dude. I was impressed. And I completely understood why our local sheriff had decided he needed to haul this alleged "human" off to the pen for the night, and why my bosses had decided to lob this case my way.

Didn't mean the guy was actually a demon or anything, but it was best to be safe in a town where all sorts of supernatural creatures wandered the streets.

I picked up the phone and called my sister, Bronwyn. "Hey. Human guy gets into a fight with four werewolves, injures three and walks away with minor injuries. What do you think?"

I heard the slurp of her drinking her coffee. Bronwyn wasn't an early riser. She'd probably just rolled out of bed five minutes ago. "Are you smoking crack?"

I looked heavenward and shook my head. "That's what the police report says. They arrested him. Clinton is pressing charges for assault."

She choked on her coffee then began to laugh. I waited patiently until she'd finished and managed to catch her breath.

"Who the hell is this guy, Chuck Norris?"

"I know, right?" I replied. "What are the odds?"

"Slim to none, that's what they are." She took another sip. "You get tagged to pull the guy's ass out of jail?"

"Of course," I replied.

"Well, be careful. Could be some Navy SEAL, ninja,

badass. Or could be someone you might not want to mess with without your amulet and a staff of power."

"Or could be a human who didn't have the smarts to back down."

"Then he'd be a dead human," Bronwyn countered.

I bit my lip in thought. "The werewolves wouldn't kill a newb. They might beat the shit out of him and toss him across the wards, but they wouldn't kill him."

"Two nights from the full moon?" Bronwyn scoffed. "Please. Someone insults them this time of the month, and there's gonna be blood."

She wasn't wrong. "So why isn't this guy in the hospital, and why is Clinton whining about being assaulted?" I mused.

"Because maybe he's not really human?" Bronwyn replied. "Cass, be careful. I enchant objects. All we've got in Accident is a bunch of wards surrounding the town that haven't been updated in decades. Those things do their job, but if someone's carrying around an enchanted object, or if they're not really a human, the wards aren't going to negate that."

"You thinking a VanHelsing?" I asked.

"I fucking hope not. But be careful, just in case."

I thanked her and promised to make that coconut cream pie she liked for Sunday dinner, then hung up, digging the amulet out of my purse and draping it over my neck before getting my jacket, and heading out to the door to the county lockup, to see someone who might be the son of the devil, and hopefully get him out on bail.

CHAPTER 3

I stood outside the cell and gave my client a quick look-over. His mug shot hadn't done him justice. Even with the black eye and a cut along his jaw, the guy was panty-dropping hot. He had blood all over his torn shirt, and crumpled, mud-stained gray trousers, all of which somehow made him even more attractive. The guy had bad boy written all over him, from the wavy lock of dark brown hair that fell across his forehead to the emerald green eyes that were busy appraising me as I appraised him.

Yep. Hot guy. I doubted he was a demon, though, or he wouldn't be bruised and cut. If a werewolf could heal those kinds of wounds within hours, I'd assume a demon could do the same. Actually, I'd assume a demon wouldn't even get bruised or cut to begin with. But then again, I'd locked all those books up in the attic when my grandmother had died and not bothered to read them since the funeral. What I remembered about demons wasn't enough to fill a thimble.

"Witch."

I blinked, wondering if I'd imagined the whispered word or his look of astonishment.

"What?"

"Are you my breakfast?" He gave me a lazy grin. "If so, I hope they remove these handcuffs."

I glanced down, surprised that they'd left the cuffs on him. Huh. Sheriff Oakes wasn't usually so paranoid. There must have been something that made him think a jail cell alone couldn't hold this guy, or that he might be a danger to the magical beings that ran the detention center.

Demon. He had beaten the shit out of one, actually two, werewolves. But he looked so human here in this jail cell, with the handcuffs and the bloody shirt, and that rakish, sexy smile on his oh-so-handsome face.

The man got to his feet and prowled over toward me. My blood quickened and I swallowed hard. Shit. This was so unprofessional. How long had it been since I'd gotten laid? Too long, evidently.

"Mr...." I looked down at the folder in my hand, even though I'd pretty much memorized the contents. "Mr. Doe. I'm Cassandra Perkins, the lawyer that's been assigned to you. To…help you."

"Can you get these cuffs off me, Cassandra?" he purred. "I'm not exactly sure what sort of help you're going to provide to me, but let's start with these handcuffs."

He might be human, but I got the impression this guy was still dangerous, so just in case I touched the amulet under my shirt, and straightened to my full five foot, eight inches. Wards. Laws. And if the guy tried anything, Bronwyn's birthday gift would ensure it would be the last thing the fucker tried.

"Put your hands though the bars so I can reach the cuffs," I told him.

He did so and I eyed my sister's handiwork. I might have refused to do magic, but my siblings didn't have the same reticence. And Bronwyn was a damned skilled witch.

I took a breath and muttered a word, reaching between the bars to touch the handcuffs. They fell free into my hand, and I slid them through to my side of the cell. It was a simple spell, but I'd felt something quicken inside me the moment I'd said the words. The man on the other side of the bars must have felt it as well because he caught his breath.

He still seemed human, even without the magical handcuffs. Human, but with the magnetic sexual attraction I'd never felt for humans. I blamed it on growing up in a town where over ninety percent of the residents were "other" beings. That attraction made me wary, made me wonder if he really was human, or something else.

I cleared my throat. "As I mentioned, I'm here to represent you. You're being charged with two accounts of second-degree assault, drunk and disorderly, and vandalism." I flipped through the file. "Drunk and disorderly I can probably get dropped. Pete's no stranger to that at his place. Vandalism…the owner of the truck isn't thrilled about their windshield, but they're also not a fan of werewolves. If you're willing to shell out a few hundred to replace the windshield, she'll probably let it go."

"I don't have a few hundred." He was continuing to stare at me, his gaze intense. I felt hot, flushed. And I was really wishing there wasn't a row of enchanted metal bars between us.

It was probably a good thing there was a row of enchanted metal bars between us.

"What can I offer her?" I asked, trying to concentrate on my lawyerly duties. "The two assault charges…well, that's going to be more problematic. But I think I can play the werewolf-two-nights-from-the-full-moon card if the other charges get dropped."

"I don't have any money. And why are those werewolves pressing charges? It's not like they didn't hit me back."

"Says here you started the fight. Do you deny that? Mr….Doe?" For fuck's sake. That wasn't the guy's name. He needed to start being straight with me if I was going to defend him.

"I did start the fight. He was being an ass. The guy deserved to be taken down a notch. It was good for his soul. Humility might save him from an eternity in hell."

Here we go. Here comes the psycho shit. "We've got a couple of choices here. You can plead guilty and embarrass the werewolves, thus pressuring the prosecutor into a lesser charge on a plea. Stanley, the guy with the broken arm, will do whatever Clinton tells him to do. I make the werewolves out to be a bunch of pansies, losing a fight to a newbie, I mean a human, and they'll fold."

He nodded, gripping the cell bars with his hands and leaning close to me. "And the other choice?"

I leaned close as well, fully cognizant that what I was about to propose would cost me my license in any town but Accident. "You post bail. You leave town. You never come back."

He blinked, that slow, sexy grin creasing his cheeks. "Isn't that against the law? A warrant for failure to appear? Bail bondsmen and the police hunting me down? I like how you think, Cassandra, I'm just a bit surprised that my lawyer is advising such a thing."

I clenched my teeth. "I'm advising scenario one. Scenario two means I need to get the charges dropped before you have to appear."

"And if you don't get the charges dropped?"

I couldn't exactly tell this guy that the moment he crossed the wards, he'd forget everything he ever saw or did here in Accident, that our police wouldn't cross county, or state, lines to hunt down a human for something so minor as getting the upper hand in a fight with a group of werewolves.

I couldn't tell him that although we based our laws on the neighboring human ones, we bent those rules a lot—a whole lot.

"Let's get you out of here on bail, and worry about all that later, after I talk to the prosecutor." I grimaced, not exactly looking forward to talking to the prosecutor. I hadn't seen Marcus…well, I hadn't seen him since The Incident.

"Sounds good to me." He stepped back from the bars and eyed the lock.

I went to call the officer and hesitated. "So you don't have any identification, and you don't have any money?"

"Just this." He reached into his pocket showed me something that looked like a brass slug. "Think this will pay my bail?"

I frowned. How did he have that? The police should have taken all his personal belongings away. Someone in a holding cell, especially someone deemed dangerous enough to still have handcuffs on, shouldn't have a coin in his pocket. Or anything else in his pocket.

"I doubt the court will take Chuck E. Cheese tokens for your bail payment," I told him.

"Well, this is all I've got. And I kind of need it to get home. Charon doesn't take credit cards, you know."

"Charon?"

"The ferryman?"

Ah yes. "The ferryman". His limo-driver to hell. He was still sticking with the whole I'm a demon thing. Not that I was completely convinced he was human. I was reserving judgement on the whole thing. So far all he'd done was get drunk and beat up a bunch of werewolves. Not exactly demon behavior—or what I imagined demon behavior to be.

"So Charon, your Uber driver, takes Chuck E. Cheese tokens. Good to know. And he's coming back to pick you up when?"

The man frowned, looking at the coin before shoving it back into his pocket. I wondered again how he'd managed to keep it. I'd have to have a word with the sheriff about this.

Or not. It wasn't my business. I was a resident, not someone in charge of anything but my own damned life for a change.

"I don't know how to call him. Usually I touch the coin and call and he appears, but when I did that last night, nothing happened. This town is...weird. It's like there's something blocking me here."

A chill ran down my spine and I gave him a sharp look. My ancestor had set up the original wards around the town which my sisters and I reinforced every few months or so. It kept the peace, to a certain extent. And it did dull the abilities of our supernatural residents as well as block paranormal communications in and out of the town.

It also fucked up the cell signals. We were working on that.

Human? Or demon? Or something else? It shouldn't matter. He was a client to represent, but someone I really needed to know.

"So you expect me to believe you're really the son of the devil? That you came here for...what? To tie one on after a tough day torturing adulterers in the fifth circle?"

"Adulterers are in the second circle. The fifth is for those consumed with the sin of wrath, a personal favorite of mine." He stretched his arms above his head and looked up at the ceiling. "You really should study up on this. As a lawyer, you'll most likely wind up in hell. It's good to arrive with a solid knowledge of the layout and tortures you'll be enjoying."

Right. "I'll take that into consideration, but for now, let's concentrate on your situation here, Mr. Lucien."

"Just Lucien."

"So Lucien, walk me through what happened last night. You arrive here from hell for an evening of relaxing fun. Alone. Why Accident? Were you driving through and just wanted to stop for the night? Is there a reason you picked our town and Pistol Pete's?"

He shrugged. "Paris is so out this year? All the celebs are heading to Pistol Pete's. I'm all about following the trends, you know."

I looked at my watch. "Should I come back tomorrow? Would another day in this jail cell make you more inclined to seriously answer my questions and stop wasting my time. Time, I might add, that I'm not getting paid for?"

He smirked. "This is where Charon took me. The places I usually go just didn't appeal to me. I was bored. I wanted to try something new, so I told Charon to pick, and this is where I ended up."

Huh. That's what happened when you let the Uber driver decide where you were going to party for the night. You wound up drunk and fighting it out with a werewolf and his friends, and then in jail.

"So the Uber guy, this Charon, dropped you at Pistol Pete's?"

"Yes. A group of fairies propositioned me in the parking lot, but a satyr told them to beat it and took me inside to buy me a drink. He went off to screw a nymph, and I made my way over to the werewolves."

I took a breath. The wards meant that residents of Accident felt safe walking around as nature intended them to be. It also meant this town wasn't all that safe for newbies, humans, who didn't know the rules. We had human residents, but the newbies were always one insult away from getting a minotaur horn up their ass.

"I'm assuming things didn't work out well between you

and the werewolves. So you had a few drinks, then you got into a fight outside?"

"The fight started inside, but the manager guy kicked us out. I wasn't inclined to comply, but the others were. The guy had a towel."

I knew exactly what that towel was because my sister Bronwyn had enchanted it for Pete herself. I wasn't really that thrilled about a bar owner having something that could pretty much Taser a supernatural into a convulsing mess, but it did stop a lot of fights.

Fear the towel.

"Clinton Dickskin says you started the fight."

Lucien snickered. "Dickskin. Seriously? I think I'd change my name."

"When you're strong enough to bench a tank, no one makes fun of your name." Actually, everyone made fun of his name, we all just did it privately.

He leaned against the bars, his dark eyes meeting mine. "Yes, I started the fight. I would have finished it too if that sheriff hadn't shown up with some knockout stick. I'm not a fan of law-enforcement people. They remind me of angels, and I really don't like angels. I'm not so sure about this town either. My eye hurts, and this cut stings, and I can't manage to get out of this cage or call Charon and I couldn't incinerate that Dickwad guy with a snap of my fingers even though I tried. It was an interesting evening, but I'm ready to leave. Well, I *was* ready to leave until I saw you, that is."

Flirt. Too bad he was a client.

I looked down at my file, thinking about the circumstances of the case and what angle I should take to make all of this go away.

No money. No ID. No last name or residence beyond the "hell" scrawled on the paperwork. But Clinton had been in more fights this year than I had fingers and toes, and the guy did appear to be a newbie, which worked in his favor. Hmm. "Let me see if I can get you out on your own recognizance. If the district court commissioner says 'no', then is there someone you can call to post bail?"

"Sweetheart, if I could call someone, I wouldn't be in this jail cell right now."

Flirt.

"Call me sweetheart again and you can sit here for the whole weekend." I waved for Officer Watts to come in. "Let me do the talking, okay?"

This dude was smoking hot, but my job was to get Lucien out of this cell and out of Accident. Assault two. Drunk and disorderly. Property damage. Shouldn't be too hard to get this all dismissed if I spent my Friday night smoothing feathers around town. If I could get everyone to drop the charges, then this man could go back to hell, or wherever it was he came from, and I could get back to my normal life.

It was an ideal solution, but somehow the idea of my normal life was unusually depressing.

CHAPTER 4

LUCIEN

A witch. My blood quickened at the thought and it was all I could do to keep from reaching through the bars and touching her. It had been nearly three thousand years since I'd seen a witch, but even taking that into consideration, my reaction to her was far from normal.

Beautiful. Smart. Confident. And her energy called to me with the strength of a siren's song.

No wonder my infernal powers were blunted. A witch. A real witch. A powerful witch. No doubt that weird electric feel I'd had as Charon and I had entered the town limits had been some sort of wards. We were particularly susceptible to witch magic. It all made sense now why I hadn't been able to fry that werewolf, or instantly heal these wounds, or break out of this jail cell and go home. This explained everything.

Well, except for my coin not working. I had a feeling that had something to do with Charon, that rat bastard. I might not kill him when I got back, because this *was* turning into an interesting sort of vacation, but I did intend on making him suffer mightily for ignoring my call.

When I got back. I eyed the gorgeous witch and thought that I might just want to stay here for a few more days. Hell, I just might want to stay here forever.

As soon as I got out of this stupid cell, I was going to…

Going to what? I hadn't seen a witch in three thousand years. How did one go about wooing a witch in these times? I doubted bringing her a dozen goats and the head of her enemy would work. Or maybe it would. We didn't often have to do the wooing. Usually it was the witches who summoned us and told us what they wanted in exchange for what *we* wanted.

I just had to find out what she wanted, then propose a deal—a deal that also involved her naked in a bed with me.

The policeman who'd locked me in this cell came in, jangling keys in his hand. He proceeded to have an argument with the witch, insisting the handcuffs go back on before he opened the door. His eyes had glowed like the werewolves, but I got the feeling he wasn't a wolf. Maybe a rat from the way his nose twitched at me, but I wasn't one to judge.

This town was so fascinating. I'd been all over the world, but never had I seen such a concentration of non-humans, boldly walking around in their natural forms. Yeah, there was something weird here blocking my powers. Yeah, my bruises and cuts hurt, and seemed to be taking an inordinate amount of time to heal. Yeah, I was pretty sure Charon had set me up as payback for something I'd done in the past. But I was still having the time of my life here.

Especially now that I'd met this witch.

I eyed the woman in front of me. Cassandra, she'd said her name was. Cassandra. It was a powerful name for a powerful woman, and it made me wonder if she had any of the prophetic ability of her namesake.

That dark red hair, the way she bit her lip as she thought. The flush that rose on her cheeks when her eyes met mine. I wondered about that slim body under the suit, followed the v of her shirt neckline to the faint hint of cleavage. She was gorgeous.

But my attraction to her wasn't just that she was a witch or that she was beautiful. She treated me with the sort of confident authority I'd only experienced from two of hell's denizens—my father and my mother. Although outside of that confidence, she seemed to be nothing like the two that had given me life. Lucifer was…well, Lucifer. My mother, Lilith, was the demon equivalent of a praying mantis. She was vicious, violent, and she liked to kill those she had sex with. My father was the only exception and that wasn't through any lack of trying on her part. Actually, this witch reminded me a bit of the angels I'd encountered here and there in my life. She was sharp, single-minded, with a biting sort of humor that normally made me want to start slicing wings. Except in her, it was a bit of a turn-on.

Okay, it was a lot of a turn-on.

The police-rat must have been convincing because the cuffs went back on before he opened the metal jail cell door. He gripped my arm with white-knuckled nervousness as we followed Cassandra down a hallway and into a room. Rat-cop pushed me into a chair and Cassandra took the seat beside me.

"Did you check him?" The bald man seated behind the desk asked.

I decided to be silent and let her talk, as she'd requested—less because she'd demanded it of me and more because I was curious where all this was going. Well, and I really wanted out of that cell, and for someone to take these damned hand-cuffs off me. My call to Charon clearly wasn't getting through, and he was just the sort of asshole who wouldn't come look for me if I failed to call him. No, I would end up rotting in that horrible cell for a few years before someone needed my input on something and tracked me down. Best to keep my mouth shut and be smart about this whole thing until I figured out how things worked in this town.

And figured out how to convince this witch I was the demon she wanted to spend her life with.

"Check him?" Her voice rose and she touched her necklace. "No. Why would I check him?"

"Because…" the bald man looked at the file. "He says he's the son of the devil."

Cassandra rolled her eyes and threw her hands up in a dramatic move that had me biting back a grin. "You're kidding me, Aaron. One of the Dickskins beat the crap out of him. Does that sound like the son of Satan to you? He looks like he got run over by a truck, and he's spent the night locked behind iron bars. At best he's drunk or high. At worst, he's off his meds."

The bald guy snorted, then looked up at me. "What's your last name, son?"

Son? I choked back a laugh. "I don't have one, *dad*. I was given the name Lucien."

He glared at me. "Where do you live?"

"Hell."

"And your parents are…?"

"Lucifer, the Prince of Darkness, the Morning Star, the Infernal Master of Hell and All Who Reside There, and Lilith, the Dark Mother."

"Lucifer. And Lilith," the bald man repeated. "And you're Lucien."

I shrugged.

"They had a thing for the letter L I guess?" he asked. "Couldn't just name you Robert or Steve or something?"

"My father chose the name. He would have named me Lucifer after himself, but it would have caused confusion in hell, and Junior doesn't sound menacing enough for the son of Satan."

Bald Guy glanced over to Cassandra who shrugged. "See? Human. Crazy. And it's not like everyone in this town isn't secretly wanting to knock Clinton Dickskin to the ground."

He snorted then turned back to me. "If I release you, you need to reappear for the trial, unless your attorney works out a plea deal with the prosecutor."

"They're seriously going to continue with this?" Cassandra asked.

The bald man nodded. "Dickskin is furious, and that guy who had his arm broken might file charges as well." He turned to me. "No getting out of this one, Junior."

I continued to keep my mouth shut and tried to incinerate the man. I had as much success as I had in trying to incinerate that werewolf.

"For Christ's sake, Aaron," Cassandra snapped. "He has no money, no family. He can't post bail, and these charges are ridiculous. You know Clinton probably started the whole thing. And Stanley probably deserved that broken arm as well. How many times have you guys intervened in fights between Dickskin's gang and the others in town? This is a regular thing with those wolves, especially this close to the full moon. I'm not going to let my client, an innocent newbie, sit in jail for weeks over what in a wolf pack is a minor dust-up."

"I get it, Cassie. I do. But I can't exactly send a deputy to hell to pick him up if he doesn't show up at his hearing," the bald guy retorted. "The guy has no last name, no ID, and no earthly address. What am I supposed to do?"

"Release him on his own recognizance and trust me to get these bogus charges dropped. I'll handle it."

The bald man eyed her, slowly raising an eyebrow.

"You're telling me you're going to finally grab the family broomstick and take charge?"

Cassandra flushed. "I'm a lawyer. This guy is my client. I'm going to do my job—the job I chose. The one I went to school to do. The one that doesn't involve a damned broomstick."

Bald guy looked disappointed. "Well then, Lawyer Perkins, your client can stay here as our guest until he produces proof of a valid earthly address as well as one thousand dollars bond."

Suddenly this vacation was looking a whole lot less interesting. Normally I wouldn't care about a jail cell, but if they kept these cuffs on me, I wouldn't be able to escape. Actually, I wasn't sure I'd be able to escape if they took the cuffs off me. The memory of that officer's stick from last night, and Pistol Pete's Towel of Doom, along with the knowledge that my powers and abilities were pretty close to nonexistent made me eager to stay as far away from that jail cell as possible.

"He doesn't have a thousand dollars," Cassandra argued.

"Well then he's staying here until the hearing. Which given that today is Friday, will most likely be Monday or Tuesday."

"You keep him here, and you'll regret it," she snarled, her energy beginning to coil around her hands. I stared, fascinated. Turned on. And very aware that of the three of us, I was probably the only one that could actually see her magic.

Bald Guy's eyes narrowed. "Regret it how, Cassie? Because I'm pretty sure you're not threatening the town magistrate with bodily harm."

She glared back at him. "Forget about coming to Sunday night family dinner. No porkchops for you this week. And forget about borrowing the boat over Memorial Day weekend too."

"Cassie, that's not fair!" he shouted, rising to his feet.

My eyes went back and forth between the pair. Clearly from their familiarity and first-name usage they knew each other on more than just a professional basis, but family Sunday dinner? There was no resemblance that I could see. Was he an in-law? A distant cousin? A neighborhood kid she'd gone to grade school with that was almost an adopted part of her family? He better not be her boyfriend or fiancé, because this witch was *mine*.

Well, I hoped she'd be mine. If I ever got out of these handcuffs, that is.

She sighed, reaching up a hand to rub her forehead. "You're right. I'm sorry. But you've got to see how ridiculous this whole thing is. He's a newbie. Just let him out. And I'll… I'll deal with Marcus. I'll get the charges dropped."

That last bit was said between clenched teeth, as if her idea of dealing with Marcus involved decapitation or possibly evisceration.

The bald man gave her a sideways glance, as if he was thinking along the same lines as me. "You don't know demon-boy's address, or even his last name. The man has no ID or money. But somehow if the charges don't get dropped, you're personally going to ensure that he'll show up for his hearing?"

She sucked in a breath and sat back in her chair.

Bald guy smoothed a hand over the top of his head. "Tell you what, Cassie, I'll let him go if he'll wear an ankle bracelet —one of Bronwyn's ankle bracelets. And he needs to attend at least one anger management meeting before the hearing."

"I don't want him at that meeting," she shot back.

"Cass, if this thing ends up going to court, it's in his best interests to have been attending the meetings. He's your client. Stop with the knee-jerk reaction and think about how it will benefit his case."

She muttered something about stupid meetings, and why the werewolves weren't made to attend them. "Fine. The meeting, but not the anklet. Since when does a newbie require one of Bronwyn's ankle bracelets?"

"He wears one of Bronwyn's monitors, or he stays in jail, or he posts bond. Pick one. I'm not taking a chance that he vanishes off to hell, and I end up with Marcus and the entire Dickskin pack trying to take my head off."

Cassandra blew out a breath, balling up her fists. "Fine. Fit him up and let's get out of here before everyone starts closing up early for the weekend."

The bald man picked up the phone and barked out a few orders, then shot Cassandra a sheepish smile. "So pork chops on Sunday? And the boat…?"

"Not sure you want me making food for you right now, Aaron. Or loaning you the boat. Call me tomorrow when I've had time to settle down."

He nodded. "That temper, Cassie…you need to mind that. It's not appropriate for a defense attorney to have such a short fuse, especially someone with your…talents."

I hid a grin, hoping that I got to see some of her talents before I left town.

"Witch. Bitch. There's a reason those words rhyme, Aaron." She winked at the man, clearly her volatile temper the type that burned hot and fast, just as quickly receding.

"Just stay away from Marcus, okay? Otherwise the son of Satan won't be the only one in an ankle monitor."

A slow grin curled her lips. "Now Aaron. You know it takes more than a piece of metal to restrain me, even metal crafted by my very skilled sister."

The man flushed red, quickly looking down at the paper-work he was stacking with fumbling hands. "Oversharing, Cassie. I don't want to hear about your kinky stuff. Just don't kill Marcus. Perkins or not, we'll have to haul you in if you do."

That grin remained. "Yes, sir."

And those two words were just as much of a turn-on as the magic still snaking around her arms and hands.

CHAPTER 5

CASSANDRA

*L*ucien had been strangely silent throughout the whole exchange with the district court commissioner. Yes, I'd told him to let me do the talking, but I hadn't really expected him to comply. Mentally ill with delusions? Possibly. Or maybe he really was some sort of lesser demon. Either way the man stared at me the whole time as if he were undressing me with his eyes, as if he wanted to do a whole lot more than undress me, whether my third cousin was watching or not.

Aaron was an anomaly in our family. Ever since Temperance escaped the stake in Salem and dragged her paramour through the wilderness to found our town, we Perkins women had been the unofficial government here. Women, because only the female descendants of Temperance could inherit the "gift". Thankfully girls accounted for ninety percent of the births in our family line, with boys a mere ten percent and many of them not surviving past infancy.

That meant that any surviving boy children were doted on and spoiled. For their entire lives. Aaron was my third cousin, but we had him over for our family dinner on a weekly basis, and treated him as if he were an overindulged younger brother. The man was seven years older than me, and I couldn't help but baby him. And in all honesty, he enjoyed it. It was probably one of the reasons he wasn't married at the age of forty.

There were other reasons, but those were personal and not mine to divulge.

Deputy Hollaran brought the box and sat it on the desk in front of me, backing away. I'd have the privilege of being the one to open the box and attach the ankle monitor. There was a key that Sheriff Oakes had, and I was pretty sure Aaron had access to it, but when it came to magical items, if there was a witch in the room, handling them defaulted to her. Part of that was as a form of respect. Part of it was due to safety.

Most of our magic was fairly predictable, but Bronwyn wasn't known for her light touch when it came to enchanted objects, and these anklets were crafted to keep a giant from leaving the city limits, so they weren't exactly mundane objects as far as magical energy went.

"What is that?" Lucien's voice cracked like a whip, startling me a bit.

"An ankle monitor. It restricts you to the town limits until your hearing, which if I can't get the charges dropped, I will make every attempt to schedule for Monday. Tuesday at the latest. You won't be able to leave town while you're wearing it."

"Or what? I blow up? Sargent Handy here comes out with a stick and shoots fireworks at me?"

"No, you just can't leave the town limits." I bent down and snapped the silver band around his lower leg, feeling a jolt of electricity as I touched him that had nothing to do with the magical device. When I looked up, I saw a rather calculating look in his eyes.

"It's Friday," he said. "I have to stay in your town for three to four nights with no money? Where am I supposed to stay?"

"Homeless shelter?" I shot back. We didn't have a homeless shelter. And as annoyed as I was with this whole situation, I couldn't make this guy sleep in an alley or a field. Besides, the residents would complain, he'd get arrested, then I'd have even more work to do. "I'll see if one of the hotels will put you up for the weekend."

Hotel. Singular. We had one hotel, and I wasn't sure Bernadette and Hollister were going to let someone stay there free of charge, especially someone who was wearing one of Bronwyn's ankle monitors and was awaiting trial for assault charges and more. Although neither of them were fans of the Dickskin clan. I might be able to leverage that.

"I could stay at your house." His voice was smooth as silk, with all the innuendo.

"No."

"Sleep on the couch?"

"No." I stood up, realizing I was far too close to him. Damn, he was taller than I'd thought. And he had a lean type of wiry strength that was sexy in an elegant, classy sort of way.

Classy. With blood-stained, torn, crumpled clothing, a black eye, and a puffy, cut lip. But he did come across as classy. Arrogant classy. Entitled classy. The privileged sort of classy that said he'd spent his whole life hearing nothing besides "Yes, Sir". And here I thought Aaron was spoiled.

"You're coming with me," I told him. "To the only inn we've got here in Accident. I'll get you a room there for four or five nights."

And who knows what I'd have to promise Hollister to make that happen.

* * *

"No." Hollister scowled. "We're booked up."

"You're not booked up," I scowled back. "Come on. Four or five nights. Just until the hearing." Because after that, this guy would either be on his way out of town, or in a jail cell.

"No, we're booked up. Lisa Morgan's wedding is this weekend, and all her guests are staying here. And I don't like the idea of some felon staying in my hotel."

"Accused felon," I shot back. "Innocent until proven guilty."

"Accused, convicted, I don't give a shit. If he's so dangerous that he needs one of Bronwyn's ankle monitors, then he's not staying here." Hollister shot the other man a quick glance. "What's his deal anyway? He a fairy of something?"

Lucien grinned. I waved at him to keep quiet, but he ignored me.

"I'm a prince of darkness, the firstborn of—"

"He beat the crap out of the Dickskin boys." I said, hoping that was enough to gain Hollister's cooperation.

The older man's eyebrows shot up. "Which ones?"

"Stanley and Clinton. Clinton's not a good loser so he's pressing charges."

"Friday night. That's all I've got. He needs to be out of here by noon tomorrow."

I threw up my hands in exasperation. "Tomorrow is Saturday. His hearing won't be until Monday at the earliest. Can't you double up Lisa Morgan's relatives or something?"

"Out by noon," Hollister repeated. "And I won't charge you on account of his whupping Clinton Dickskin hard enough that he went crying to the police."

Crap. What the heck was I going to do with this guy after tomorrow noon? There was only one way out of this—I needed to go get Clinton to drop the charges. And Stanley to drop the charges. And Pistol Pete to drop the charges.

Out of those three, I dreaded the conversation with Clinton the most. I could barely keep my temper with that guy on a good day. How I was going to smooth talk him into letting this all go this was beyond me.

"Thanks. I'll take it," I told Hollister, figuring this was better than nothing. I grabbed the outstretched key, then motioned for Lucien to follow me.

"We actually do have fairies in this town," I told the man. Fairies were vicious little creatures, who liked to magically glamour themselves to appear full-sized vicious creatures. Although I was pretty sure Lucien thought that Hollister was questioning his sexual preferences.

"I know, remember? A group of them tried to pick me up outside that bar last night." He laughed. "Would they have been the ones in jail if they'd chewed me to bits? Or do you all only incarcerate those you assume are human in this town?"

"Fae have their own laws, as do the shifters and the other creatures in town." I shot him a quick glance. "Humans are off limits. That's one of the rules everyone needs to abide to continue to live here."

"Funny. No one seemed to let the werewolves know that little fact," he commented. "So this town of yours, Accident, is a haven for supernatural beings? A place where they can let their serpent-hair down and be themselves?"

I laughed. "Exactly. And Accident has been like that since the seventeenth century when it was founded."

"By a witch," he said.

I stopped walking and turned to him. "How did you know that?"

His dark eyes met mine and he took a step closer. "You're a witch. I can see the magic around you, feel the power of your energy. Only a witch of great power could manage to keep the peace with all these beings living here together.

How did you survive the inquisition? The trials? The burning times? Was there a demon who protected you? One you bonded with?"

I took a step back, not understanding what he was talking about and a bit unnerved by it all. "I'm only thirty-three years old. My ancestor, Temperance Perkins, survived the burning times, but she died centuries ago. And as for the town…we have a human system of government now. There is no witch running things here."

His eyebrows shot up. "Then what do you do here in Accident, Cassandra Perkins? What does a witch with your power do?"

Not magic, if that's what he was implying. "I'm a lawyer. I'm a resident. I live here just like everyone else. I pay my taxes. I vote. And I don't do magic."

He frowned, clearly puzzled. "What do you mean you don't do magic? I can see your energy. You're a witch—a powerful witch. You should be running this town."

I abruptly turned away and kept walking toward the room. "I have no desire to do magic, or to run this town. Right now the only thing I want to do is to get you settled into this hotel room, and try to get the charges against you dropped before everyone heads out to happy hour."

"Judging by the fact that you're holding a real key with a plastic tag saying number six on it, I'm going to assume this isn't an upscale place," Lucien commented drily as he followed me to room six.

"Not the Hilton," I told him, unlocking the door and motioning for him to enter with a sweep of my hand.

He stepped inside and turned slowly around, taking in the room. "Not the Motel Six either."

"It's clean. No bugs or nasty stuff. Just a simple inn, and far better a choice than anything else you might have."

"No so," he told me with a grin.

"What, sleeping in a field or on a street corner is better than this?"

"I meant your house. That's a much better option."

I let out my breath in a frustrated whoosh, thinking that if I didn't talk Clinton Dickskin into dropping the charges, that might be where this guy ended up after noon tomorrow. Why hadn't I just let him stay in jail over the weekend? Why had I bothered to insist that he be released? And why in the hell had I personally guaranteed he'd show up at his hearing?"

Because he'd seemed so out of place there in that cell. It had seemed wrong somehow. And whether the guy was crazy or an actual demon, he'd still gotten the upper hand on Clinton Dickskin. That had to be worth more than a weekend in jail.

"Television remote is over there." I pointed to the dresser. "Towels and linens are in the bathroom and that closet."

"And the food?" He eyed me. "I'm assuming there's no room service?"

Crap. Double crap. The guy had to eat, and even if I managed to get the charges dropped, he still probably hadn't had any real food since last night.

"No, but I'll call for a pizza delivery." And have to pay for it out of my own pocket as well. This case was bringing a whole new meaning to the term pro bono.

The corner of his mouth quirked up. "Will you be joining me for this pizza? Perhaps delivering it yourself?"

"Nope. Stay here. Watch TV. Eat your pizza. I'll be back tomorrow before you need to check out."

Hopefully I'd be back before then. Hopefully.

* * *

THE PIZZA ENDED up costing me nothing. It seems Hollister

wasn't the only one thrilled that Lucien had pummeled our town bully. For assaulting a werewolf, the guy was getting a large hand-tossed with the works and extra cheese. I wondered how many freebies would be delivered to Lucien's hotel room door once the word of his deeds spread throughout the town. He'd be a bit of a legend.

Maybe I could use that in getting the case dropped.

I took the winding road out of downtown, heading up Heartbreak Mountain and turning down a narrow private lane. Originally the wards had only encircled the town proper, but over the last two centuries, it became clear that as our population grew, the area we warded needed to as well. Any supernatural who lived outside the wards was vulnerable. Inside, their abilities and skills were blunted, but they were safe. Any human encountering them would find their memories altered once they were out of the town limits.

Which meant when Lucien left, the knowledge that Clinton wasn't human, that the anklet he wore was magical, or that the girl delivering the pizza was a banshee would fade away. Accident would just be a small mountain town where he'd gotten drunk and fought some guy, luckily escaping with only one night in jail and all his beautiful teeth still intact.

If he was human. If he was actually a demon, he'd remember it all. I shivered wondering about the implications of that. We'd never had demons in Accident and until now I'd not questioned that fact. Maybe foundational wards kept demons out, and that portion of the spell had degraded? As much as I hated the thought of dragging those books down from the attic, I might just have to do some research.

Actually, I didn't hate the thought. Something in me thrilled at the thought of going through those books, of crafting spells as I'd done all through my childhood. I remembered my mother helping me with my first charms, standing beside my grandmother as we reinforced the wards, sabbat in our back yard every week. A part of me missed that.

And a part of me resented that I'd never been given a choice in all of this.

But there was possibly a demon in our town, and that might mean I'd need to get over my sulk-fest and put on my pointed hat—hopefully temporarily.

Was he a demon? The other supernaturals had blunted powers, but his seemed to be far more than blunted. It was as if he'd been nulled by the wards. Did they affect demons more than the others who called Accident their home? Or was he in fact just a human who'd had some sort of psychotic break and thought he was a demon? Perhaps the werewolves had hit him a bit too hard in the head and this was a result of some concussion.

Either way, I hoped the sheriff had at the very least given Clinton a stern lecture. I'll admit I was more than a bit pissed that he hadn't hauled the werewolf in along with Lucien. Yes, the Dickskin family lawyer usually got Clinton out of jail so fast that I doubted the werewolf had spent more than five minutes total in a cell the last year, but there really needed to be some sort of consequences for this sort of thing. Clinton Dickskin, all of the Dickskin pack actually, had taken to behaving as if this town was their own. They threatened the locals, squeezing some of them with a protection racket. They fought with visitors and townsfolk alike. They got angry when they didn't get their way and keyed cars or peed on people's shrubberies. And let me tell you, nothing kills a shrubbery dead like a healthy dose of werewolf pee.

Something had to be done about these Dickskin werewolves, and I wasn't sure our sheriff was the one to do it. There were plenty of supernaturals in this town, including other shifter packs, but no one wanted to challenge the Dickskins.

Which meant this was eventually going to fall in my lap. I swallowed hard, thinking of any possible way out of this. Seven prime witches lived in Accident—all of us descendants of our founder. Seven sisters. We were close. We were all of a generation. And the responsibility for the town had fallen to us.

And we'd done nothing. Actually, I'd done nothing.

In our defense, this wasn't the same town or country it was back when Temperance and her lover set the first wards around a tiny cluster of houses. We had a democratically elected mayor. We had a sheriff. The Perkins witches only needed to make sure the wards held, not go around policing the behavior of the residents.

Or did we? Because if we didn't, who's to say one day there wouldn't be a murder, or something more serious than a drunk-and-disorderly? Who's to say one of the Dickskin pack might decide they wanted more than just some spare change, free beers, and to always win at poker? We'd been just fine in Accident the last three generations, but there was an unsettled feeling in my gut that our peace might be ending. That it might already have ended. And my intuition told me the first step to reversing this was to put the fear of God into Clinton Dickskin and his family, and get that newbie holed up at Hollister's out of town. And to do it before nightfall.

CHAPTER 6

CASSANDRA

Clinton's father, Dallas, answered the door. I'm pretty sure he would have slammed it in my face had I been some random person there selling magazines or soliciting donations for the local volunteer fire department, but I had two things going in my favor—I was a witch, and I was female.

Actually, I was pretty sure the last thing was the reason he didn't slam the door in my face.

Not all the daughters of witches had magical ability, and of those that did, quite a few couldn't manage more than a very specialized area of spellcraft. Some of us really got the short end of the magical wand—boil water with a touch, but only a few cups at a time, call an object from across the room, but only if that object weighed less than three pounds and wasn't more than twenty feet away, invisibility, but only from twilight to dark and only if she had the forethought to put on camo or dark clothing first.

My sisters and I had a wider range of skills and abilities. None of us liked to completely show our hands, but being a descendant of Temperance Perkins meant the town residents, supernatural and otherwise, tended to regard me with caution. Well, they regarded me with caution after The Incident anyway. Before that, no one paid much attention to me at all.

Dallas was far more interested in what was between my legs than any magical power I might or might not have. He'd always been a letch. Didn't matter whether someone was a werewolf, a harpy, a ghoul, or a witch, if they had boobs and a reasonably appropriate slot B for tab A, then he was game.

"Dallas. I'm here to talk with Clinton about what went on last night." No sense in beating around the bush with this guy. Small talk would only give him the impression that he had a chance to get me in his bed in the next hour.

He leaned against the doorjamb and tossed his silver hair over one shoulder, stroking his reddish-blond beard with one hand. All the werewolves had long hair, men and women both. Men and the occasional woman also had an ample supply of facial hair. I think it was less to do with grooming trends and more to do with the fact that werewolves grew hair at an alarming rate, especially around the full moon. Their healing ramped up this time of the month as well. Last year Evie Howler had fallen face-first into a bonfire during one drunken party and come out of it looking like something from a horror movie. The next night not only was her skin completely healed, but her hair had grown back to past her chin.

"Sure you're not here to see me instead?" Dallas continued to stroke his beard.

"Unless you're the one pressing charges against my client for assault, then no." I squeezed in past him and immediately regretted it as the guy copped a feel on my ass.

I'm a witch. I could have hexed his hand or cursed the thing right off his wrist joint, but I didn't practice magic, and I needed this werewolf's cooperation. For all his skeeviness,

Dallas was pack alpha. I wouldn't go so far as to sleep with him, but if grabbing my rear got him to insist Clinton drop the charges, then so be it.

"Clinton's pretty pissed," he told me. "Who the hell beat him up anyway?"

I shrugged, moving out of the range of the werewolf's hands. "A newbie. Some tourist."

He chuckled. "Some tourist? You see Clinton's face? And Stanley wound up with twenty stitches in his head along with that broken arm. If he'd been human, he'd probably have been dead."

I grimaced. "Stanley is the one who got his head shoved into the windshield, right?" Dallas nodded. "Well, if it's any consolation, the guy in jail doesn't look all that good either."

Actually, he looked pretty damn good, and I wasn't just talking about how attractive the man was. I'd seen people who'd been on the other side of Clinton's fists before and it hadn't been a pretty sight. Last month a werewolf had come close to killing one of the humans in town. We let the werewolves get away with a lot, but serious injury and death was where we drew the line. The sheriff had asked us to visit the pack compound as a group and make it quite clear to Dallas that the werewolf clan needed to follow the town rules. I'd been bouncing that stuff back on our elected officials for over almost two decades but for some reason I was in a bad mood and had decided to intervene. I'd marched up to the compound and told the alpha that the if someone died, every wolf in town would wind up a rug on our floor. Normally Dallas would have laughed in my face, but ever since The Incident, he'd seemed to take me a bit more seriously. Since The Incident everyone took me a bit more seriously.

Temperance Perkins hadn't established this sanctuary and put these protections in place for supernaturals to turn into a bunch of bullies. Maybe Aaron was right. Maybe the town did need a witch to keep things in order. But why did that witch have to be me?

I know. Whine, whine, whine. But seriously, could I at least have ten or so years of my life where I didn't have to do something that was imposed on me because of who or what I was? Or because someone else wasn't up to the task?

"Well, Clinton's spitting nails," Dallas commented. "That guy might be a tourist, but he's no newb. Man took on four werewolves and lived. What the hell is he, Cass?"

Like most supernaturals, Dallas underestimated the abilities of non-magical humans. And he underestimated how vicious a crazy person could be when provoked. Still, I couldn't help but wonder if Lucien really did have something demonic going on.

Or he was just really kick-ass at fighting.

"He claims to be the son of Satan." I shrugged and held up my hands. "If that's the case, Clinton and the boys are lucky they walked away at all from that fight."

Dallas' reaction was just as comical as his come-hither routine had been. The werewolf shuddered, his blue eyes wide. "A demon? I hate those damned things. Why you gotta let them in town, Cass? Why can't it just be us here and the occasional newb and tourist without a bunch of hellspawn mucking things up?"

I blinked in surprise, and not just because he felt like I was the one that decided who got to stay in Accident and who got to leave. He'd encountered a demon before? There'd never been a demon in Accident as far as I knew. And as far as I knew, Dallas had spent his life here, outside the occasional hunting vacation in the Rockies or up in Alaska. Where had he encountered a demon? And why was he so worried?

"We've got to be welcoming to all sorts, Dallas," I told him. "This town was founded to be a haven to all. If we're going to open our wards to werewolves, gargoyles, mermaids, and silkies, then we need to let demons in as well. If you feel otherwise, then petition the mayor, not me."

"You're the witch," he countered. "You're the eldest female of the line. You're the one that decides this stuff, not some jackass of a mayor."

"Times change," I informed him. "We're not living in the seventeenth century any more. I might be a witch, but I'm not the duly elected official of this town. If you want to ban demons from Accident, take up a petition or talk to the mayor."

"Don't want them here. They don't belong here. Demons aren't like us," he complained. "I don't feel safe with one in town. I don't trust that your magic can keep him under control, make him mind the rules, ya know? And when witches and demons get together…well, it ain't fair. It ain't at all fair."

I tried to sort through his words, trying to determine what exactly was fueling his objection.

Would a demon be something that a town full of paranormal creatures and an entire coven of witches couldn't control? And the thought made him, a huge powerful werewolf alpha…scared?

Scared. What on earth could possibly scare Dallas Dickskin, the alpha of Accident's werewolf pack? Certainly not a guy who'd been locked in jail overnight, contained by metal bars and still sporting some rather impressive bruises and cuts. I was pretty sure my sisters and I didn't even scare Dallas. He'd promised to keep his werewolves in line more in the hopes that he'd get one of us in the sack than any respect toward our local law enforcement or my recent threat to haul their hides to the local taxidermist.

Who was a leprechaun. Seems tanning hides and

preserving the dead was a particular skill of theirs. Who knew?

I eyed Dallas with renewed interest. "Well, newbie or demon, I can't kick this guy out of town and hex him into never returning if he needs to stay here pending a hearing on assault charges," I pointed out. "Aaron made me put a spelled ankle bracelet on him just to make sure he didn't skip out."

Dallas made all sorts of expressive facial expressions and began once more to stroke his beard. "I'll talk to Clinton," he told me.

"Why don't *I* talk to Clinton?" I countered. "Or better yet, both of us talk to Clinton?"

He nodded, then lifted his face to the ceiling and howled. It was a deep, guttural sound, far more hair-raising than the calls I'd heard from actual wolves and coyotes out west. This vibrated from deep in his throat, filling the house and my ears with the type of melodious note that both made my heart lurch with the beauty, and my skin prickle with fear.

I was pretty sure he'd just hollered for Clinton, but like all families, others came running as well, no doubt to see what sort of trouble the black sheep of the Dickskin family had gotten himself into. They kept a respectful distance, but by the time Clinton stomped sullenly into the room, the walls were lined with a dozen other werewolves, all trying to look like they were doing something benign while stealing quick curious glances at Dallas and me. I recognized a few of them, having grown up here in Accident. Besides the few I'd seen around town, I saw Stanley, his arm mended enough that he didn't need a cast, but still sporting a line of half-healed stitches across his forehead. By his side were two other bruised werewolves who I assumed had also been involved in the scuffle at Pistol Pete's last night. A few feet away was Shelby, the only female wolf who was actually in the room instead of lurking in the hallway. She was leaning against the wall, her arms crossed, a smirk on her face. Or maybe it was a sneer. With Shelby, it was hard to tell.

"What?" Clinton's snarl was the second thing that raised the hair on the back of my neck in the last five minutes. I had to hold myself back from clutching the amulet around my neck.

"Drop the charges," Dallas snapped back. "Don't want no demon in this town, and the witch can't kick him out if he's gotta be here to stand trial. So drop the charges."

"He's not a demon." Clinton came dangerously close to his alpha, looking the elder man square in the eye. "He's just some newbie who's got an attitude."

Dallas looked pointedly at the yellowish-purple of Clinton's faded bruises. "Telling me some newb did that?"

Clinton actually blushed. Embarrassment? No, now that I looked closer, I think it was an angry sort of red that suffused the werewolf's face.

"I'd had a bit too much to drink or they'd a been hauling him out of town on a stretcher."

"Four of you had too much to drink?" Dallas laughed. "Poodle. I've got newborn bitches that fight better than you."

I sucked in a breath realizing that not only had I lost control of this situation, but I was probably about to witness a fight the magnitude of which the town hadn't seen since Dallas killed Old Dog Butch and took over the pack back in '68.

I breathed out a word and traced a quick sigil in the air, feeling the power surge through me milliseconds before the flash-bang lit the room and made every werewolf in it yelp. A few of the werewolves ran into the safety of the hallway. Dallas and Clinton froze where they stood. Shelby's eyes widened and she watched me with barely concealed alarm.

I felt a momentary weakness, a rush of exhaustion, like someone had opened up a drain and let all my energy out before quickly replacing the stopper. Even the slightest magic had a cost. But this minor fee was well worth the attention and respect it gained me here in this room.

Ignoring the alpha, I turned to Clinton. "I got stuck representing this newbie. Or demon. Whatever. And I really don't care who started the fight, or who-put-who through the windshield of a truck. I've got a tourist in town with no money and no identification. I'm having to put him up in Hollister's inn on my damned dime because you're embarrassed that someone got the jump on you in a fight and like a puppy, you went whining to the law. Drop the charges. I'll have the guy out of town by nightfall. No one ever needs to hear how a newbie, a tourist who apparently has no magic whatsoever, managed to land more than one blow on a werewolf."

It was a risky tone of voice to take with a dominant male werewolf, but I'd found out over the years that playing this bunch involved a whole lot of bravado and a whole lot of bluffing.

The air crackled with tension. I could practically hear the werewolves around the edges of the room say a low "ooo". Clinton sucked in a breath and glared at me, while I forced my hands to not clutch the amulet at my neck.

Temperance Perkins had allowed the first werewolves into town in 1723. In the outside world, they'd been hunted nearly to extermination. The bonded pair who'd begged for sanctuary were with a pack of only six others. They were so starved that they looked like gaunt corpses. The female alpha had been pregnant, her tiny belly the only bit of flesh on her skin-and-bones body. She'd confessed to Temperance that she'd lost a litter earlier in the year, and that all her previous pups had been slaughtered by their first adult full moon.

Let no one ever say that witches didn't have a compassionate heart.

Temperance not only let them into the town, a sanctuary she'd created that had up until this point housed only witches and the humans who were sympathetic to their plight, she went on to allow other shifters in as well. She'd allowed fairies and pixies, mermaids and sirens, ghouls and chupacabras. And more. She'd been a tight-laced, stern, God-fearing religious pilgrim who'd been cast out and nearly put to death by the people she'd loved just because she had a gift of magic. And that event had been the catalyst that opened her Christian heart to allowing others refuge in the sanctuary she'd created. Over the centuries the tiny wolf pack had accepted other refugee werewolves and grown to their current size, taking over the entirety of Heartbreak Mountain, and causing the witches to expand the town limits considerably to ensure their safety. They owed us. And by us, I meant the town. Clinton dropping the charges, and allowing his pride to be just as bruised as his face was the right thing to do for the town. And for the pack.

"No," Clinton snarled. "I'm not dropping the charges. Newbie or demon, I agree that man don't belong here. I want him gone, but it's the rule of our land that people pay for what they've done. He struck first. He put Stanley though a windshield and broke his arm. He's gotta have his day before the law and pay by spending time in jail. Maybe he's a demon. Maybe he's just a crazy newb who's really good at fighting. Either way, man's gotta pay."

Since when did Clinton Dickskin give a damn about anyone paying? Oh, silly me. Clinton was always concerned when it was someone else who had to pay. Not so concerned when it was him who was being called to account.

"He spent the night in jail, Clinton," I told him, my tone more conciliatory than it had been before. "He looks like hell from the fight. He spent the night in jail. And now he's holed up at Hollister's with no food and no change of clothes and no money for pay-per-view. He's wearing a magical ankle bracelet because Aaron wanted to make sure the guy who didn't have any ID and no apparent fixed address managed to make it to his hearing. Just drop the charges. Let this dude limp home and never come back and take whatever psych meds he needs to be on to remind himself that he's not a demon or the son of Satan. Drop the charges."

The werewolf met my eyes, then looked back at Dallas before turning to me again. "Not now. Not tonight. The hearing will be Monday or Tuesday. I got some things I gotta work out this weekend, and I'll think about it. Come see me Sunday night and I'll let you know."

That wasn't good enough. "How about you let me know tomorrow noon?" I asked, thinking of Lucien's check-out time and how I had nowhere else for him to stay after that point.

Clinton narrowed his eyes. "Meet me at ten for breakfast at the Stagecoach tomorrow morning, and we'll discuss it. If I'm so inclined, that is."

I winced, hoping that maybe he might be so inclined if his bruises were completely healed by then, and if he'd somehow managed to regain his status in the pack after a disastrous bar fight. Whatever. It might be easier to smooth the guy's ego after he'd slept and when he was away from his pack and facing a stack of cinnamon-spice pancakes with extra whipped cream.

"You've got it, Clinton," I told him. "And if you decide to drop the charges, breakfast is on me."

CHAPTER 7

CASSANDRA

It was closing in on five o'clock by the time I got down from the mountain where the werewolves had marked their territory. It was too late to work on those trespassing cases, even if I'd brought the paperwork from the office with me.

Happy hour? Or…

Crap. I turned down Cherry Street and pulled into the parking lot behind the Lutheran church, making it inside right at five thirty. Martin smiled at me and opened the book next to him, putting a check mark next to my name while I sat down and tried not to fume that I was the only one here that wasn't "anonymous". It was my temper that had gotten me here in the first place. Being an angry attorney was par for the course. Being an angry witch attorney was evidently something that could cost me my license and my job if I didn't get it under control. I had no idea how my boss would explain to the bar association the reason he was recommending my disbarment, but I was sure he'd somehow manage it. Was anger-fueled magical activity in the courtroom technically illegal? It wasn't like I'd pulled a knife on someone.

Besides, it had been my ex-boyfriend. My ex the prosecutor. My ex that I somehow needed to convince to drop this case now that Clinton was digging in his heels.

My ex who in spite of what I'd done, still wanted to get back together with me. Which was so not happening.

Martin looked over my shoulder, beaming a smile at whoever had come in behind me. "Welcome! Have a seat. We're just about to get started."

A familiar voice returned the greeting, making the words sound like smooth decadent barrel-aged bourbon. I turned in surprise to see Lucien lowering himself into a chair next to me. He scooted it over a few inches and I scooted away a few more.

The man had somehow managed to find new clothing. It fit. It fit really well. And unlike the usual jeans-and-t-shirt that most men around town wore, he was looking like he was about to board a yacht in a pair of khakis and a crisp button-down shirt. Still hot. Still someone who needed to get out of town yesterday, and not be hanging out at a twelve-step meeting for people with anger management issues.

"What the hell are you doing here?" I asked.

"Now, Cassie," Martin scolded. "Everyone is welcome. And I'm sure our newcomer will tell his story in a moment, if he's feeling like sharing. If not, that's okay. All in the twelve steps, you know."

I wanted to punch Martin in the face. Lucien grinned, his eyes dancing with laughter. "Didn't that magistrate man agree to let me out without a bail if I wore this ankle monitor and attended anger management sessions? Well, here I am."

John Cotton, our resident cyclops chuckled. "Dude. You're the guy who took on four of the Dickskin clan single handed. Heard you gave that poodle Clinton a shiner that he's still trying to heal from."

The others in the room sucked in a breath and began to clap. John stood up and shook Lucien's hand. Great. The nutjob had become a local celebrity.

"Did he start it?" Alberta asked, her already huge eyes even wider.

"Don't answer that," I told Lucien. It was probably a good thing I was here. These meetings were supposed to be confidential, but I knew all too well how gossip spread in a small town. I was having a hard enough time getting Lucien off the hook for last night without him bragging about his pugilistic abilities and getting Clinton Dickskin even more riled up.

"What I want to know is what landed *you* in these meetings," Lucien asked. "I mean, not that I'm surprised or anything, I just want to hear the details."

"Well, you're not going to hear the details," I snapped, determined that I wouldn't be sharing at this meeting, or any other meetings until this man was clear of town.

"She set her ex-fiance's pants on fire," John told the other man.

"He deserved it," Alberta added. "Liar, liar, pants on fire, you know."

"Setting someone's pants on fire in the middle of the courtroom was the problem," Martin added. As if doing the same thing out on the street or in the privacy of one's own home were perfectly okay.

Lucien's eyebrows shot up and he gave me an appreciative once-over. "I think I'm in love. Did you burn the offending body part off his body? Third degree burns? Oh, please tell me that he died."

"No, he didn't die." What kind of witch did he think I was? "And I didn't burn anything off. Just a bit of blistering, and that was only because he was wearing polyester pants.

Edith grabbed the fire extinguisher and put him out within seconds."

The expression on Lucien's face was damn close to setting me on fire—certain parts of me at least. "That's… that's the hottest thing I've ever heard."

Um, pun intended? I wasn't sure with this guy. I wasn't sure anything with this guy. His whole "I'm the son of Satan" thing was the sort of psychosis that would undoubtedly think that setting an ex on fire was a good thing.

And if he really was a demon…well, that explained a lot.

"Probably would have been worse if he hadn't been a panther," Alberta added. "Means he heals fast. And he thinks that sort of thing is hot too, although he wasn't too pleased about it at the time. Actually, I think he was more upset at having fire extinguisher foam all over his crotch than having his pants burned clear off his body."

John chuckled. "I was there. Made it look like he stepped out of a bubble bath. Or his dick exploded. Either one."

"You a panther?" Alberta eyed Lucien appreciatively. "They like it rough, you know. I like it rough. Just thought I'd let you know that."

Alberta was a troll. Her kind of rough would kill Lucien if he were really a human. Actually, her kind of rough might kill Marcus as well. Shifters were sturdy, but not troll-sturdy.

"Is a panther like a male cougar?" Lucien asked with a puzzled frown. "Like older humans who prefer sexual partners much younger than they are? I'm not particularly attracted to younger demons when it comes to sexual partners, but of course any humans are obviously much younger than me. So I guess I *am* a panther."

Alberta sent him what was probably supposed to be a smoldering glance. I fought the urge to grab my amulet. Pissing the troll off would have consequences I didn't want to contemplate but I didn't want her injuring my client.

"Wanna get it on later?" she purred. "Got a place under the bridge I like to do my business at."

I kicked Lucien's ankle and shot him my best horrified look, shaking my head. His look in return was definitely smoldering.

"Going to have to pass, ma'am. There's someone else whose bridge I'd like to be crawling under tonight."

I choked back a retort, and tried to resist setting the man's pants on fire. It wouldn't be a good move in the middle of my anger management meeting. And if he were a human, I'd end up breaking my own rule and killing him.

Alberta pursed her lips. "Shame. Good looking man like you could do a lot better than a witch like Cassie. She might like the rough stuff, but witches still break easy, ya'know? I'm more sturdy. And better looking."

Lucien's gaze hadn't left my face. "Like it rough, do you *Cassie?*"

"Ms. Perkins," I corrected, my face on fire.

"Obviously," Alberta replied, "or she wouldn't have been thinking about getting married to a panther. Or thinking that setting his pants on fire at work would set his heart on fire as well."

I hadn't been trying to get Marcus back. What kind of freak gets turned on by that sort of thing?

The freak next to me, obviously.

"Can we get started?" I asked irritably.

"Yes, let's get started," Lucien drawled. "I've got a bridge to breach. Let's get this meeting underway."

Martin gave us all a benevolent smile. "Who would like to start?"

John raised his hand, then adjusted the patch he used to cover his not-eye. It helped that his actual eye wasn't exactly dead center. The patch just made it look like he had incredibly close-set eyes and wasn't a cyclops. John hated that thing, but it gave his face a symmetry that he lacked without it and kept any newbies from staring. And as much as John hated the patch, he hated people staring at him even more.

"Went to the grocery store on Tuesday," he announced to our little group.

Alberta, Martin, and I clapped, while Lucien seemed perplexed that a trip to the grocery store would warrant such enthusiasm.

"Excellent!" Martin told the cyclops. "How did it go? Did you achieve your goal?"

We left each weekly meeting with self-assigned goals. John's was to make polite conversation with strangers and have an outing in public without getting into an argument with any of those strangers.

"I said 'thank you' to the cashier."

We clapped.

"I didn't yell at the man in the produce section for tasting the strawberries."

We clapped.

"But I did get into a fight with a man who didn't return his shopping cart to the corral."

We collectively held our breaths.

"You scolded him?" Martin asked hopefully.

John shook his head, fingering the patch once more. "I was polite, but he gave me the finger and told me to fuck off, so I grabbed the cart and started smashing it into his car. I didn't hit him though. And I didn't eat him, although he looked tasty. Better than that rump roast I had in my shopping bag."

"You should have crammed him into the shopping cart, set it on fire, and rolled it down a hill," Lucien commented.

"Not helping," I muttered.

"Or eaten only his toes, to teach him a lesson. Proper punishment is key to behavior modification," he continued.

"Do you *want* to go back to jail?" I snapped at him.

"Now, Cassie," Martin scolded. "Let's communicate the rules to our newcomer in a calm, peaceful manner." He turned to Lucien. "We're here to help each other control our anger and more violent impulses, not encourage them. What do you think John should have done instead of damaging this man's car?"

"A non-violent punishment?" Lucien tilted his head in wonder.

"A non-violent solution?" Martin corrected.

Lucien shifted his feet, the anklet coming into view just below his pants hem. "Lock him in the car with the windows up and not allow him to leave for a week?"

"That's illegal," I told him. "How about John returns the cart to the corral himself, uses his breathing techniques to calm his emotions, then eats some chocolate?"

That wasn't what I'd do. Or what I'd try to do. In reality I was more in line with John's way of dealing with the situation, but I'd learned from three months of these anger management meetings to parrot the party line.

"Or eat the rump roast raw," Alberta suggested. "He could imagine he's eating the rude man and cool his temper that way. That's what I'd do."

Martin pursed his lips. "It's a good coping technique, Alberta. As long as you're confident that you won't cross the line into actual cannibalism."

She sniffed. "It's not cannibalism if they're human. Not like I'm eating other trolls or something. Yuck."

"No eating the humans," I reminded her. "Or the elves or the mermaids. Packaged grocery-store meat only."

"The Dickskins hunt deer," she complained.

"They have a permit," I reminded her. In all fairness, Alberta had never eaten any humans or other town residents. Her biggest problem was that she was horny and not a lot of men seemed willing to have sex under a bridge with a troll, no matter how drunk. Well, maybe if they were *really* drunk, but that sort of thing usually didn't result in a repeat occurrence or even a text the next day. Hence Alberta's anger management issues. None of us liked rejection, but Alberta really didn't like rejection.

"I've got it," Lucien announced. "Follow the man around all day, singing a jingle on repeat. Something really annoying like that Meow Mix one."

"Or the Hefty, Hefty, Hefty chant?" Alberta asked.

"The Oscar Meyer song?" I suggested. I'll admit, the idea had merit.

"Folgers?"

"That Empire Carpet one?"

"Chili's baby-back ribs?"

"Ooo, ooo," I bounced in my seat. "The Kit-Kat jingle. He'll never get that out of his head." I hummed the tune. Anger management meetings had never been so much fun.

Martin frowned. "Maybe during the actual confrontation, but I don't think it's a good idea to follow someone around singing a jingle at them all day. Such an act might end up in a violent altercation."

"But we wouldn't have started it," John protested. "Finishin' is okay. Starting is not."

"Finishing is not okay," Martin told him. "Nonviolence, John. Step away from any attack. Don't meet violence with violence. That's what we're working on here."

I clamped my mouth shut and nodded, trying to be a good attendee. Two more months of this and I'd be done. Well, done attending meetings, that is. I'm not sure my setting my ex-fiancé on fire days were over for good.

"Let's give our newcomer a chance to share." Martin turned to Lucien. "If he wants to, that is."

Lucien sprawled back in his chair, a lazy grin creasing his

cheeks. "I'm Lucien, son of Lucifer, and I'm here because the bald man told me that I needed to come as part of his conditions for letting me out of jail."

"Your dad's name is Lucifer?" John shook his head. "Man, that sucks. Who the hell would do that to a child?"

"My grandfather," Lucien told him. "Because my father was the light of his life until he got opinions of his own on how to run the family business. There was an epic fight. Tore the whole family apart. They're still not speaking with each other."

Alberta made a sympathetic cluck noise. "Have you ever met your grandfather? Sometimes it takes the next generation to bring a family feud to an end."

Lucien shook his head. "I've been kind of busy running our end of the family business. When dad split, or was thrown out depending on whose story you believe, he took his side of the business with him. Used to be the whole thing ran as a single enterprise, heaven on one side, hell on the other. Now they're completely split apart. No communication whatsoever. It's a problem, in my opinion, but there's really nothing I can do about it. Until the two old men decide to make peace, it's one side or the other."

I'd been totally intrigued, envisioning a big family business like a cannery, or excavating, or fishing, until Lucien had mentioned heaven and hell. The other three were nodding, as if Lucien had used the terms as a metaphor, but I knew better. The nut job really did think he was Satan's spawn, and I guess grandpa was God or something.

Unless...

Such a shame, because either one was a deal breaker. Maybe. I could change my mind about that because the man was damned hot. I'd totally do him. And I wouldn't set his pants on fire afterward either. Well, maybe not.

"So you work for your father in his end of the family

business?" Martin asked, tapping his pencil against his chin. "I'm assuming based on what you've said about your relatives, that anger management issues run in your family? Your father has a hot temper?

Lucien snorted. "Hot is the understatement of the year. Everything pisses him off. It's always 'my way or the highway' with my father. My grandfather is the same way, although I hear he's better about his temper lately. Still a controlling asshole, but less likely to smite you or set shrubberies on fire to prove a point."

"You can break the cycle," Martin urged. "You don't have to be like your father or grandfather. You can choose to walk away from the violence you were raised in."

Lucien looked rather stunned at that pronouncement. Then he turned to me. "What about your parents?"

John laughed. "You kiddin? Seven daughters running around hogging up the bathrooms? You betcha there was a lot of yelling in that house."

"Actually, there wasn't," I corrected him. "Not much yelling at all." Not much of anything at all. I glanced at my watch, willing the time to go faster because I really didn't want to talk about my family. When Grandma had died, everything had sort of fallen apart here in Accident.

"Her mom lit out after the elder witch bit the big one," Alberta spoke up. "Dad wasn't ever in the picture by the time the youngest was born."

"Your dad fathered seven children and left?" Lucien scowled.

"I don't want to talk about this."

"Is he dead? Because I can track him down in hell and make sure he receives some extra suffering."

"He's not dead and I don't want to talk about it."

"And when did your mom leave? Seven kids." He shook his head. "No wonder you've got a short fuse."

"I don't want to talk about it," I told him with enough firmness in my voice to get my point across without sounding so angry that Martin was forced to make a note on his paper.

"Let's hear more about Lucien, then. Tell us about the fight." Alberta leaned forward eagerly. "I want to hear about you beating the shit out of Clinton Dickskin."

"No, we do not want to hear about that," Martin interjected. "It doesn't further our objectives here to dwell on the details of our loss of control. I'd rather Lucien tell us how he felt before, during, and after the incident."

I sat back, thankful that for once the attention wasn't on me. I'd gone over my feelings far too many times in prior meetings. Time for someone else to take a turn under the microscope.

Lucien blinked at Martin, then turned a puzzled frown toward me.

"Go on." I was going to enjoy this. "Tell us all about your *feelings.*"

"I wanted to hit that man from the moment I saw him," Lucien began.

"No surprise there. We all want to hit Clinton Dickskin," John interrupted. Martin shushed him.

"But I'm not on the clock. I mean, really I'm *always* on the clock, but when I pop out of hell, I try to not worry about coming up with creative punishments that are appropriate for the level of sin."

"You just wanna relax with a drink, and maybe find someone hot to drag home under the bridge." Alberta sighed. "I totally get that."

Martin turned his shushing her way before smiling encouragingly at Lucien. "So what was it about Clinton that set off these impulses in you? Let's start with that."

Again with the puzzled frown. "He's a sinner. You're all

sinners, but he's the kind of sinner that calls out for punishment."

Was it horrible that my mind had suddenly taken a hard right turn into the gutter. I was a bad, bad girl, a naughty sinner in need of punishment from a naked Lucien. I'm not the type that had ever been into getting tied up or spanking, so the punishment I was envisioning was him pounding me into the mattress. I looked over to Alberta and realized she was thinking the same.

"No." I said.

The word came out with an edge of a snarl that had Martin putting his pencil to the pad. What was wrong with me? Yeah, I was a bit possessive when it came to my boyfriends, but Lucien was a client. A tourist. A newb who was going to be out of town come Monday—Tuesday at the latest. Yes, I was beginning to wonder how unethical it would *really* be if I banged my client, but that didn't mean I had to get all up in Alberta's face about it.

I didn't run this town. We had an elected mayor, an elected sheriff. Grandma had been the last Perkins witch to govern our fair city. When she'd died, our legacy had died with her. If Mom didn't give enough of a shit to stick around and run things, let alone parent her daughters, then it wasn't my responsibility either. Helping raise the seven of us was enough work. This town wasn't my responsibility—well beyond keeping the wards functional, that is. And that was just as much for my benefit as for any supernatural creature here in Accident.

"Sorry," I told Alberta. I meant it.

She smiled, and my heart ached a bit at the sadness there. "No problem. Backing off. All yours, witchy-girl."

My face heated with embarrassment both that she knew exactly what my emphatic "no" had meant, and that now the guys in the room did as well. Well, maybe not John or Martin who were giving the pair of us blank looks. Lucien did from the sexy grin on his face.

"Really? I'm hoping that means I won't be spending the night on that lumpy hotel mattress. Or maybe you'll be joining me on the lumpy mattress?"

Electricity arced through me at the thought. Client. Client. I needed to keep reciting that like a mantra before I ended up in bed with this guy.

"Nope. Not gonna happen. Keep going with your story, hellboy."

He sighed dramatically. "I resolved to ignore the werewolf, knowing that his time would come, but his behavior was so…annoying that I finally had to take action."

"You hit him? Threw a drink in his face? Set his pants on fire?" Alberta had been obsessed with my pants-on-fire curse ever since the news of it had left the courthouse and spread through the town like…well, like fire.

"No, I told him to leave. He threw a drink in my face, then threw a punch. The rest is a blur, although I do remember us somehow taking the fight outside. And I remember three of the guy's friends joining in when it was clear he was getting his ass handed to him." Lucien cracked his knuckles, a grim, determined glint in his eyes that seemed not quite human. Not quite human, or maybe just crazy. It was hard for me to tell the difference anymore.

"Once control slips from your fingers, it's often difficult to rein it back in," Martin commented, beginning a speech that I'd heard before—one that ended with suggestions to use breathing techniques, time-outs, or even calling a sponsor to avoid becoming embroiled in a fight. Lucien nodded, but he seemed to be giving the man's lecture the same lack of attention that the rest of us were doing.

After that I listened to Alberta tell us all how many men, and women, she'd propositioned in the last week, and how she'd not reacted to each rejection by dragging her victim off under her bridge for non-consensual sex. Alberta needed to get laid. Her last…boyfriend, for lack of a better word, had been a minotaur. I thought they'd been well suited, but after a few months, the bull decided to leave town for a sabbatical roaming the country impregnating some hot Angus bovines. He'd never returned and Alberta had fallen into a depression that was turning into an increasingly frantic search for true love, or at least a good roll in the hay. Or moss. Or gravel. Or whatever substrate was under her bridge.

My, that sounded naughty.

"So, Cassie, it's your turn." Martin smiled at me. "Tell us what challenges you had this week?"

"It's six!" I announced, jumping to my feet. "Great session, Martin. Thank you. I feel much calmer already. I'll share on Tuesday, since we're clearly out of time." Tuesday. After this pesky Lucien was gone. I'd probably have a lot to share since part of getting him out of town would involve dealing with my ex-fiancé. Hopefully I wouldn't set his pants on fire this time. Or stab him. Or sleep with him.

Sleep with him. Must not sleep with Marcus. I'll admit, it had been difficult keeping that from happening since our break-up. He was a panther shifter and like Alberta, I was a woman with needs. And thinking about those needs had me giving Lucien a side-eye that was hopefully not full of smoldering desire

Client. Client. Don't sleep with Marcus, and don't sleep with the client.

Everyone stood and we recited our non-religious version of the anger-management serenity prayer, then headed outside.

"You up for happy hour, devil-spawn?" Alberta shot me a quick glance. "You too, Cassie?"

"Lucien should go back to his hotel room and keep out of trouble," I told her. "I need…I need to go see the prosecutor."

"Marcus." Alberta drawled. "That panther you used to shag."

Her eyebrows wiggled, but it was the sudden heat I felt from Lucien that had me pivoting toward him in surprise. Was that a spark of crimson in his dark eyes, or a reflection from the sun?

"You gonna burn him or screw him?" Alberta asked.

The air was suddenly ten degrees hotter. I eyed Lucien suspiciously. "Neither. I need to convince the prosecutor to drop the charges against my client here. Then I'm going to call Lucien an Uber and get him out of town."

"My ride isn't responding," Lucien reminded me. "I've tried, remember?"

"It might not be your usual driver, but I'm pretty sure I can get you a ride," I told him.

"To hell? I doubt that," he scoffed.

"To wherever the hell you want to go," I informed him. "I'll even pay. I just want you out of my town before noon tomorrow."

My town? It wasn't my town. I mean, it *was* my town in that I lived here, but not because I was a Perkins witch, or because I was the eldest Perkins witch. Nope. Not my responsibility. Let the mayor and the sheriff take care of things. All I needed to worry about was keeping my job, and not setting my ex-fiancé on fire. Oh, and the wards. That too.

"I'm coming with you."

Yes, there was definitely a glint in Lucien's eyes. What if he really was a demon? The son of Satan? I fully believed that demons existed, but not that one, especially one who was the son of the devil, waltzed into my town, got into a fight with a werewolf, and spent the night in county lockup.

"You most definitely are not coming with me," I told him.

"Your ass is sitting on a lumpy mattress at the hotel. All night. Alone. I'll see you at noon when I come to pick you up."

That slow, panty-melting grin returned. "You'll see me before that."

Yeah, in my wet-dreams from the direction my thoughts were heading. "Hotel. Now. I need to see Marcus before sunset."

It was close enough to a full moon that the shifters in town got rowdy when the daylight faded from the sky. For some that meant they were itching for a fight. For the cat shifters, it meant sex. And damn, Marcus was hard enough to resist in the daylight when he wasn't pouring on the hot-growling sexy-stuff. I reached up to touch my amulet, thinking once again how satisfying it had been to set that feline's pants on fire.

CHAPTER 8

CASSANDRA

I swung by the courthouse, but unsurprisingly Marcus had left for the day. That left me with several unpleasant choices. I could spend the next few hours driving around looking for him at his home and usual haunts. I could call my sister Ophelia and ask her where my ex-fiancé was. I could text him and tell him I needed to see him right now.

Ophelia's specialty was divination. The woman could find just about anything from the source of a ground spring to a set of missing keys. She could also find people. Sometimes. She was better with keys.

It wasn't her less-than-stellar track record with locating town residents that had me hesitating, though. Ophelia was a paramedic. Friday night was kind of her busy shift. By the time she found a spare hour to do the ritual, it would be well after dark. And I definitely didn't want to meet with Marcus after dark. Which was also the reason why driving around for hours looking for the panther shifter wasn't a good choice either.

"Chicken," I muttered under my breath as I pulled out my

phone. Gritting my teeth, I typed the text and hit send. Then I began to count.

Twenty seconds. That's how long it took for Marcus to respond. My heart sank as I read the text. He was at home. I should come by right away if I wanted to see him because he had plans tonight.

I was glad he had plans and hopeful that they were important enough that he'd not be tempted to ditch them and try to get me into bed. But his home… Ugh, I'd hoped to meet him in a public place where I'd be more likely to resist his come-on, and more likely to hold back from setting his pants on fire.

Oh well. I knew turning Marcus into a panther-torch didn't do anything but make him more eager to win me back, and I knew he healed quickly from serious burns and had plenty of clothing to spare. What worried me more was my will to resist the sexy feline.

Marcus lived in a penthouse condo. This was Accident, so penthouse here meant it was on the fifth floor with no concierge or private elevator. Still, I had to hit the buzzer to get in and type a code in the elevator to access the fifth floor. He opened the door wearing a towel, his dark skin and hair glistening with water. The guy was built, and I'll admit my mind immediately began to replay all the hot nights we'd spent rolling around in his, or my, bed. He smirked and flexed his chest muscles as he opened the door wider for me to enter.

"Nice timing on the shower," I told him. "You must have hopped in right after you texted me."

"I told you I've got plans tonight," he purred. "Of course, I could change those plans. One word, Cassie. One word and I'm all yours for the night."

"Lucky me." I turned to face him. "How about three words? Drop. The. Charges."

He tilted his head. "Huh?"

"Lucien. The guy who was in a fight with Clinton Dick-skin last night. I want you to decline to prosecute and have the charges dropped." Then I remembered Martin's statement about catching more flies with honey than vinegar. "Please?"

"Clinton filed the charges." He flexed again. "Ask *him* to drop the charges. Tomorrow. After you spend the night with me."

I forced my eyes to remain on his face and not his lovely, sculpted body. "Clinton won't drop the charges. Come on, Marcus. You and I both know Clinton started that fight. There were four werewolves against one newb who is off his meds and thinks he's the son of the devil. It's a bad case."

"Maybe for you. A newb holds his own against four were-wolves, sending one to the hospital? Beating Clinton Dick-skin hard enough that he still has cuts and bruises the next day? Maybe the guy *is* a demon."

"I don't care if he's a rainbow-farting unicorn, it was four against one, and you're picking on the newb. No one in this town feels one bit of sympathy toward Clinton. I'm going to have your ass if this ends up in front of a jury."

"Promises promises." He stepped closer. "You can have my ass right now. You can have any of me right now."

I suddenly realized that Marcus' determination to prose-cute had less to do with the merits of the case and more to do with getting me in his bed. Son of Satan? He had to have known they'd send me to defend the guy. And he had to have known given what an ass Clinton was, I'd need to track him down for a face-to-face. I hadn't seen Marcus in two months, even though he'd declined to file a restraining order after the pants incident. This was his way of attempting to win me back.

And it wasn't working. I'll admit, the guy was hot and we

had participated in some pretty steamy sex in our rocky relationship. Standing before the mostly naked panther shifter, I was all in admiration of his physique but that was it. Here I'd been worried that one sexy look from him and I'd be naked in his bed, when the only feelings I was experiencing right now was aesthetic appreciation.

No, when I thought of sex right now, a certain client of mine came to mind, with a crooked smile and a wicked glint in his eyes, and the soft ease of a real predator. Not this arrogant panther before me.

"I don't want your ass or any of you," I told Marcus. "I want the charges dropped and the anklet off Lucien so I can get him out of town before Clinton Dickskin decides to take the law into his own hands and get revenge for the asswhooping he got." I suddenly had a brilliant idea. "And if I don't get him out of town by noon tomorrow, the hotel will be full and I'll need to put Lucien up in my own house until his hearing."

Marcus sucked in a breath that told me he'd met Lucien in person and knew a rival when he saw one. "Sleep with me tonight and I'll withdraw the case."

My license is on the line because I set an ex's pants on fire in the courtroom, but Marcus gets away with this shit. The world was so damned unfair sometimes.

"I'm not sleeping with you." I crossed my arms, pushing my breasts up and forward. Two could play at the pectoral muscle game. "But Lucien I must admit that I'm tempted to take *him* to bed."

Yes, it would be a huge ethics violation, but so would Marcus dropping charges if I slept with him, so we were even as far as I could see.

He muttered a curse between clenched teeth. "Cassie, I'm sorry. How many times do I have to say I'm sorry? I want you back, and I'll do anything to make that happen."

"You were *never* faithful to me, Marcus. Never. And every time you'd apologize and swear to not do it again. It's over. You've slept with every woman in town, and it's clear to me that you'll continue to do it again and again. We're over. Permanently. Forever."

It had been so humiliating, the side-eye, the whispers. Marcus hadn't been discreet and I'd gotten tired of looking the fool. And now that I looked back, as fun as the sex had been, it had been totally lacking in any kind of emotional component. I had nothing in common with this shifter beyond our law degrees. I didn't like him. And all those words he'd spoken of love and devotion, the ones that seemed to fill the empty spot that a neglectful father and mother had left, now seemed hollow. Marcus hadn't lied. He really did feel those things for me. And the moment he wasn't around me, he was feeling those things for someone else.

That wasn't what I wanted. It made those empty spots seem deeper and more painful. And it made me crazy—crazy enough to set his pants on fire in the middle of the courtroom.

"I love you, Cassie," he told me.

"You love every woman you bed, Marcus." I'll admit there was a bit of sorrow and self-pity in my tone. "I'm not sleeping with you. I'm here to ask you to drop the charges against Lucien."

"Or you'll sleep with him?" The panther sneered.

"No threats. Look at this as a prosecutor, Marcus. It's a bad case. It wastes time and money, and it's going to make you look like a chump in front of the whole town."

He sighed, running a hand through his hair. The towel shifted, showing his hipbones and that happy trail I knew so well. "Fine. But I can't do anything until I talk to Clinton."

"Tonight?" I asked hopefully.

"Tomorrow morning," he told me. "It's almost full moon, and you know very well what I'm going to be looking for tonight. Since you're so unwilling to oblige, I'll go elsewhere. And in the morning, after breakfast, I'll go track down Clinton."

I felt the tension fall from my shoulders. He'd still need to run by the courthouse and do the paperwork, and things wouldn't be official until Monday, but it should be enough to get the anklet off Lucien and get him out of town by tomorrow nightfall.

He'd leave. He'd immediately forget about everything except vague memories of a drunken bar fight and narrowly escaping prosecution for assault. He'd forget about trolls and cyclops and werewolves and witches. He'd forget about me.

I'll admit I really didn't like that one bit.

CHAPTER 9

I went straight home from Marcus', feeling that sense of belonging the moment I pulled into the driveway. I'd grown up here, in this big old house that was a mishmash of a two hundred and fifty year old log cabin, two almost-as-old clapboard add-ons, and an extension out the back that housed the kitchen and provided the much-needed plumbing for both the downstairs and upstairs bathrooms. Three bedrooms and a loft meant we seven sisters never had our own space as kids, but we were close and liked sharing bedrooms. Dad had left before Babylon was even born. I was nine. Bronwyn and I remember him. Ophelia and Sylvie were five when he left and have vague memories of pancakes and pipe tobacco. For the others, it was always Mom sleeping alone in that big bedroom on the first floor.

And then the big bedroom was empty, because after Mom took off, I refused to sleep in there. I still refused to sleep in there, preferring the loft I'd once shared with Bronwyn. The eldest daughter inherited the house, and although I was pretty sure Mom and Dad weren't dead, we girls acted as though they were. So the house was mine, with its creaky floors, four layers of wallpaper, exposed electrical wires, and insane heating bill each winter.

I'd never hated this house, never blamed it for the actions of our shitty parents. It had been in my family since some ancestor had laid the first log. It had sheltered us and kept us from harm. It had its quirks, but the old place was the one thing from my childhood that I truly loved.

Well, the house and my sisters.

I shut the heavy oak door behind me and tossed my purse and briefcase onto the couch, not bothering to lock anything up. Accident was a small enough town that burglaries were rare. Besides, no one would be foolish enough to steal from a witch, even one who was reluctant to practice her arts—especially one who was famous for setting a certain panther shifter's pants on fire.

The fridge hadn't miraculously stocked itself when I'd been at work, so I found myself facing the choice of a wilted salad from two days ago, a block of cheddar, or pretending that protein smoothie was an actual meal.

"Screw it," I muttered, opening the freezer and taking out a pint of brownie chocolate ice cream. Dinner of champions.

I was halfway through the pint, my shoes off and my feet on the coffee table, when Bronwyn walked through the door. I had six sisters, but outside of Sunday family dinner, we each lived our own lives, crossing paths occasionally in the grocery store or while getting gas. Bronwyn was the second eldest, and the second quirkiest of the seven of us in my opinion—which is saying a lot coming from the witch who set her ex-boyfriend's pants on fire.

"Got a break in the wards." Bronwyn smoothed an auburn lock back from her forehead, tucking it into the elastic of her stubby ponytail and leaving a dark smudge on her tanned skin in the process. She was a welder, a part-time farrier, and was the only one of us who'd eagerly embraced her magical abilities. She'd made the enchanted device Lucien was wearing around his leg. She'd made the amulet I wore around my neck. And for some reason, she was the barometer for the wards that surrounded our town.

"How bad?" I shoved another spoonful of ice cream in my mouth, dreading that I'd need to put my shoes on again and go out. I was half a pint away from pajamas and Netflix, damn it.

"Bad enough that you need to slam that ice cream and come with me."

Crap. I ate faster. "Tree come down again? Kids messing around? Freeman's dog digging for rabbits?" None of those typical issues warranted an immediate fix though. They usually just weakened the wards in one spot, not caused an actual break. Weakening meant humans leaving town might vaguely remember mermaids frolicking in the lake. A break meant we would need to hunt down anyone passing through town and slap a forgetfulness spell on them.

Ugh, I hated doing forgetfulness spells. I hated doing any spells. Well, that *one* had been fun, but I wasn't convinced the temporary glee had been worth the last two months of anger management meetings.

"No." Bronwyn frowned. "I'm not sure what it is. I didn't want to go look at it without you along."

I got up and slapped the lid back on the ice cream. There was no sense in asking Bronwyn "why me". I knew "why me". I might not want to perform my magic, but lack of use didn't negate the fact that I was the most powerful of the seven of us. And I was the eldest. And magic grew as a witch matured. And I was the only sister whose magic was of a broad-based type. They all had specialty areas. I was the generalist of the family. So no matter what happened, I was the one best suited to take care of the situation.

There was no escaping my heritage. Well, I guess there

was if I left town like Babylon, but I didn't want to leave town. I liked it here with all the people I knew, all the supernatural beings who called this place home. I liked my house. I liked Sunday family dinners. And to be honest, there was this part of me that felt responsible for the residents here, no matter how much I tried to deny it.

So I crammed the half-eaten ice cream back into the fridge, tossed my spoon in the sink, wedged my poor feet back into my shoes, and followed Bronwyn out the door and to her truck.

We'd barely backed out of the driveway before Bronwyn started in on me.

"Sooo…, who's the incredibly hot dude stashed at Hollister's wearing one of my ankle bracelets?"

Gossip spread like wildfire in Accident, but Bronwyn was the introvert of our family and often complained she was the last to know everything.

"Newbie. Maybe a newbie. He got into a fight with Clinton Dickskin and Clinton's pressing assault charges." I kicked aside an empty energy drink can and a crumpled fast-food bag. Damn, Bronwyn really needed to clean this truck.

She burst out laughing and the sound drew a smile from me. I loved her laugh. Sadly, I didn't seem to hear it much lately.

"Oh, poor butthurt Clinton! Someone actually got the best of him in a fight for once. A newb my ass. So this guy is what, a grizzly shifter? An ogre? Half-dragon? No way he's a *newb*." Bronwyn shook her head. "If so, then I'm guessing he took a shotgun to Clinton. Or possibly a rocket launcher."

I chuckled. "He says he's the son of Satan, so a demon. I thought he was just a crazy newb. I haven't seen him do anything particularly demonic. Not that I've ever met a demon."

"Well he'd have to be Chuck Norris to be a newb and get

the best of a Dickskin in a fight. Sure he's not telling the truth? Maybe he's a half-demon or something."

"There are no half demons, just full ones," I reminded her. "If they impregnate a human, the baby is a demon or a human, not a half something." So Grandma had always said, anyway. There were books on these things, journals written by our ancestor witches and passed down through the family. We'd read them as children, slowly deciphering the swirly cursive writing and faded letters. After Mom left, I'd boxed them all up and stuffed them into the attic, determined never to set eyes on them again.

"Sounds like he did *something* demonic if he beat up Clinton Dickskin enough to get charged with assault," Bronwyn commented.

I shrugged. "Doesn't matter. I talked to Marcus and he's going to talk to Clinton and drop the charges come morning. I'll pull the anklet and have a taxi pick him up by lunch time."

Bronwyn nearly ran off the road. "You saw Marcus? Did you guys get naked? Should I be looking for a wedding registry in the near future?"

I shot her a sideways glare. "I did *not* get naked, although Marcus did answer the door dripping wet from a shower and wearing only a tiny little towel around his loins. No screwing. No getting back together. Just business, then I got out of there so he could go get ready to prowl and hook up with whatever 'ho he managed to score for the evening."

Ugh. Bitter much? Not that Bronwyn noticed. My sister was eyeing the road ahead with a lewd smirk on her face.

"Man, the idea of Marcus's loins… Damn, Cassie. You're killing me. I might need to pull over here. Wet, glistening, almost-naked Marcus…."

"I know." No sense in denying it. "But he's a total sleaze. Don't make my mistake and jump in bed with the gorgeous hot guy who fills your head with promises of love and adoration."

"Are you kidding? Promises of love and adoration? Gorgeous hot guy? Sign me up, girl! Maybe not Marcus, but I'd be happy to have some man use me, even if just for one night."

I winced. None of us were short women, but Bronwyn was a hair over six feet, and had always been heavily muscled for a woman. You'd think in a town full of powerful supernaturals, men would love an Amazon who could rock a forge and welding torch, but Bronwyn's stature combined with her blunt, tomboyish nature and loner personality meant men were more willing to sling back a few shots with her than head for the bedroom. I'm pretty sure she was still a virgin. The only one who'd expressed any sort of interest physically in my sister was Alberta. Bronwyn had thanked her and told her that as she was a "sausage and eggs" girl, she'd need to decline.

Sausage and eggs. Bronwyn was freaking hysterical with her odd dry humor. She didn't have my anger management issues. She didn't have Ophelia's depression or Adrienne's wild side. She was just as quirky and fun as the rest of us. Why couldn't some man see that in her and fall in love? Why couldn't Bronwyn ever seem to find a happy ever after?

Not that I could find a happy ever after either. Maybe we Perkins witches were cursed that way.

I reached out to squeeze her arm, thinking that the hard muscles under her shirt rivaled Marcus'. "You'll eventually find someone, Wynnie."

She snorted. "I have. He's called 'The Vibrator In My Bedside Table'. Now back to the subject at hand, there's trouble brewing with the werewolves in case you didn't notice. We need to decide what we're going to do about it."

My eyebrows shot up. "First, that was not the subject at

hand. We'd been discussing a half-naked Marcus and whether Lucien was a demon, not werewolves and their squabbles. Secondly, even if there is something going on with the werewolves, I'm not going to do anything about it. Not my problem. We have a sheriff."

"We're the witches, Cassie. This is our town. And you're the eldest. You can't dump everything off on Sheriff Oakes. The poor guy is up to his leaves in stuff as it is. The residents did a great job holding things together after Grandma died and Mom bailed, but it's not fair to ask them to continue to run this town on their own. Temperance Perkins made a promise when she set the first wards. It's our duty to keep that promise."

"No, it's not," I snapped. "I'm here. I didn't move away like Babylon. I stayed and I help maintain the wards. That's as much duty as I owe this town. I was left to raise six little girls at the age of thirteen. I'm done cleaning up other people's messes. I'm not responsible for anyone or anything besides myself. It's bad enough that the law firm gives me every case in Accident. It's bad enough that I have to run out at sunset on a Friday night, abandoning a perfectly good pint of ice cream to reset the wards that some idiot broke."

"And yet you continue to have the whole family, cousins and all, over every Sunday for dinner, just like Grandma always did," Bronwyn reminded me. "You live in the old family house in town, when no one would have blamed you for selling it and leaving. Cass, I'm grateful for all you've done. If it hadn't been for you, we would have been divvied up between foster homes across the state when Mom left. You took charge. You cast that awe-inspiring spell that convinced a family court judge to emancipate you at *thirteen* and let you be guardian to six younger sisters. I was eleven. I remember that ritual. Holy shit girl, I still get chills when I remember the power you pulled to do that."

I'll admit I had a smug sort of satisfaction when I thought of it. I'd been desperate and angry. More than angry. Full on rage, is what I'd felt when I'd realized Mom had left and the future we were facing as wards of the court. I'd poured every bit of rage into that ritual, kept our little family together, and at the age of thirteen, suddenly became an adult responsible for six children. And I hadn't come up for air until Babylon had turned eighteen six years ago.

"The town didn't expect you to do more than raise us all those years," Bronwyn continued. "But once Babylon turned eighteen, they were expecting something more from you than fixing the wards and occasionally defending a goblin or selkie in court."

"Well, they were expecting wrong." I set my jaw, determined not to let my sister guilt me on this. She was the closest to me in age. We'd shared a bedroom growing up. Of all my sisters, Bronwyn was the one whose opinion of me mattered the most. The faint disappointment in her voice was killing me, but I wasn't about to let her know that.

"Full moon starts tomorrow night," she told me. "Dallas Dickskin has challengers to his status as pack alpha. There's going to be trouble this weekend."

"Dallas Dickskin has had challengers to his pack every full moon the last six years," I replied. "As long as they don't interfere with Sunday's family dinner, they can do whatever the hell they want up on that mountain."

"Ophelia says this moon is going to be bad. She says this time it's more than two werewolves brawling in the moonlight for control of the pack. She said what happens this weekend is going to be huge. It's going to change the town forever. And you're in the middle of it."

A chill ran over my skin, and my heart stuttered. Ophelia and Sylvie were twins, so similar in appearance that even our grandmother had struggled to tell them apart. But where

Sylvie had the gift of granting luck—both good and bad—Ophelia's power was divination. It was all she had. The woman was a skilled paramedic, but when it came to magic, divination was it. Go figure that with the name of Cassandra, I couldn't divine my way out of a paperbag, where my sister rocked that skill. Sadly, her premonitions were often so vague that they were useless, but this one was eerily specific. And disturbing.

"Change the town how?" I scowled. "Like maybe the Dickskins kill themselves completely off? Or kill all the werewolves off and we no longer have to deal with their problems? Because that's the kind of change I'd like to see."

"The werewolves aren't all horrible," Bronwyn chided. "And neither are the Dickskins. A few bad apples, you know."

She was right. And I too worried that the change Ophelia had prophesized wasn't going to be a beneficial one for the town. Or for me. Why was I in the middle of it all? Did it have something to do with this mess between Clinton and Lucien?

Whatever it was, that was happening tomorrow night, where right now Bronwyn was parking off the side of a dirt lane, her headlights pointed toward a huge deadfall.

"Here?" Duh. Bronwyn knew her stuff. We'd reset the wards around this deadfall five years ago when a storm had brought down a bunch of trees. It was easier to move the wards then try to get an emergency backhoe out here to clean everything off. Hopping out of the truck, I surveyed the area, assuming the trees had shifted and dented the flow of energy.

But Bronwyn had said a break.

I walked over to the deadfall and stood on my tip-toes. It was definitely disturbed, like something large or heavy had climbed over it. If they'd knocked a bunch of branches down on the other side, it might have broken the line of sight of the wards. They were set up so a quick temporary disruption in the flow of energy wouldn't set off any alarms—so people traveling to another town, or deer roaming the forest wouldn't disturb them. Actually, the magic should have gone through trees or stones. A break? That usually meant magic. As in two incompatible magics shorting each other out.

Standing here wouldn't tell me anything. One of us was going to have to climb over this shit and check the ward. And it wasn't going to be me.

I looked down at my shoes. And at my navy pantsuit that I hadn't changed out of when I'd gotten home. "I'm not exactly dressed for scrambling over a deadfall," I told Bronwyn. "I've got my work clothing on."

"So have I."

I bit back a smile. "Your work clothing is Carhartt overalls or pants and Red Wing steel-toe shoes. Mine is a silk-poly blend pantsuit."

My sister threw up her hands. "Fine. But if my overalls get dirty, I'm sending you the dry cleaning bill."

Bronwyn grumbled under her breath and climbed her way up and over the deadfall, her work boots slipping and sliding on the wet bark.

"Got it!"

I heard her mutter an incantation, felt the electric prickle of magic, then heard the crack and snap of branches as she made her way back up and over. By the time she appeared on my side of the deadfall, Bronwyn had a healthy coating of mud on her pants and shirt as well as a few leafy twigs snagged in her hair. She also had something clutched in one hand covered by what appeared to be an old-fashioned handkerchief.

"Seriously?" I gestured at the handkerchief. "Your initials embroidered on that thing? Lace around the edges?"

"You try fumbling for a Kleenex when you're sweating

next to a forge." She opened the handkerchief and showed me what she'd found on the other side of the deadfall.

It was a coin. It looked a lot like a beat-up, old Chuck E. Cheese token.

I swore. "I left him at the hotel. How the hell did he get out here, and how the hell did he get on the other side of the ward with an anklet on?"

Bronwyn bristled. "Are you saying my enchantment failed? Because them's fighting words, Cass."

My sister took her magic seriously. I put up my hands in a placating gesture. "No, I'm just wondering if there's some magic that might have trumped yours, something powerful enough to negate what you put on the anklet as well as punch a hole in the wards."

She wrinkled her nose in thought. "It's a specialized kind of magic tailored so it's not affected by any supernatural being's gifts. I had to tweak it five years ago because Aaron found out the fae were able to remove it. There's only one loophole I couldn't close off. But if that had happened, there wouldn't have been any damage to the wards at all."

I shot my sister a narrowed glance. "What loophole?"

"The wards are like a fence, not a dome. In the seventeenth century, having them extend six feet was plenty high enough. The goal wasn't to keep supernaturals in or out, it was to keep us a secret from humans. They wouldn't know about the wards, and were hardly likely to climb a nearby tree and zip-line their way to the other side over the top of them."

I understood what she was saying. "Why don't we dome the town then? Eventually some human is going to zip-line out, or hang-glide, or fly over the town in a hot air balloon and see a bunch of pixies getting drunk at Magoo's aviary."

She laughed. "If they can see pixies from a hot air balloon, they've got some serious binoculars. Trust me, I've thought about it. Doming all of Accident and the surrounding area would take a whole lot more power than the seven of us combined would have. We just have to hope the odds of that happening are slim to none."

"I doubt Lucien can fly." I eyed the coin. "Unless maybe there were two here? Lucien flies over the ward, so his anklet doesn't keep him in, and someone else breaks through?"

"Like they were chasing him?" Bronwyn arched an eyebrow.

"Like Clinton Dickskin chasing him?" I added. "Maybe Marcus caught up with the werewolf in some happy hour bar and told him he was dropping the charges. Clinton decides to take the law into his own hands and punish Lucien. Lucien sprouts wings to get away and Clinton chases him out of town and through the wards."

"First, Clinton can run back and forth across the wards all day and they're not gonna break. Second, we've gone from 'this guy's not the son of Satan, he's a newb' to 'he's got wings'." My sister shook her head. "If he's a demon, he's not going to be running, or flying, away from a vengeful werewolf. Heck, even if he's not, a newb with enough mojo to beat the crap out of Clinton Dickskin is hardly going to flee from a fight with him."

She was right. Lucien would stay and beat the crap out of the werewolf. If Clinton had come after him, I would have gotten a text from county lockup telling me to come back and pick up my client once again.

"Let's look at this as two separate incidents and see if they meet in the middle," I told Bronwyn. "One, what could possibly cause this sort of break in the wards? Either intentional or as an unanticipated side effect?"

My sister looked over toward the deadfall. "Intentionally? Magic. Another witch, although we're the only witches in town and I don't see any of us having a reason to break the wards. Besides the seven of us could temporarily bring them down, then put them back up again if needed. There would be no reason to blow a big freaking hole through them."

"How about the guys?" Witch magic was passed down through the female line. Only daughters had magic. But in spite of that, some of our male cousins did have some special skills that bordered on a very light sort of magical ability.

"None of them have anywhere near the power to do this," Bronwyn asserted. "And we're the only witches in town."

"What if another non-Perkins witch from outside the town broke the ward?" Temperance wasn't the only witch to escape burning in the seventeenth century, and I did know a few that had come over from Europe in recent times.

"It's possible, but why?"

I held up my hand. "Let's explore that later. Right now we have the possibility that one of us did this or a witch from the outside did."

"It's not us. I would have recognized the energy." Bronwyn scowled. "I'm not going to definitively rule out another witch, but this magic feels different. I mean, another family of witches might not have the same magical feel as ours, but I get the impression whoever did this isn't human. I could be wrong, though."

Bronwyn was seldom wrong. "Okay, so what supernatural beings have magic?"

She shrugged. "Fae, obviously. Elves, fairies, pixies, nymphs—although they don't like to roam more than a hundred yards from any body of water. Maybe one of the pixies? I could see this as a prank gone wrong."

I nodded. Poor Sheriff Oakes spent more time running around after pixies then he probably wanted. I felt a wee bit guilty at the thought. The guy really *was* overworked. It's a wonder he didn't quit. I'm sure it wasn't an easy job trying to maintain some sort of law and order in a town full of super-natural beings.

That should have been my job. Well, helping him should have been my job. But damn it, why should the circumstances of my birth, something completely out of my control, pigeonhole me into a lifetime of work? For once in my damned life, I wanted to be in control of my destiny instead of doing what everyone expected me to do, instead of picking up the pieces my careless mother had abandoned. I'd already raised the children she'd left. I'd done enough of her job.

Yes, it was all about my mother. A therapist would have had a field day with me.

"Fae or an outside witch. Either an accident or for some reason."

"Let's think about possible reasons," Bronwyn said. "The wards are powerful but limited in scope. Either someone wanted to let a newb out of town with his or her memories intact, or someone wanted to have the supes inside the town limits at full power."

I nodded. The wards dampened the power of those who lived inside, to keep the peace. But there was one issue with that theory. "The effect would have been temporary. Full power for what? An hour at most until we got here to fix the ward?"

"Sounds unlikely," Bronwyn agreed. "It's probably pixies goofing off and accidently blowing a hole in the wards."

"Or someone wanted Lucien to leave with his anklet on and his memory intact."

I reached forward and took the coin from Bronwyn's handkerchief-covered hand. She gasped, then stared at me open-mouthed.

"Damn it, Cassie! Don't just go grabbing magical items!

That thing is cursed. I've got no idea what it is, but I'm glad you're not a smoking pile of ash right now."

I blinked at her in surprise, running my finger around the edge of the coin. "Cursed? I don't feel one bit of magic from this thing. Are you sure?"

Of course she was sure. Bronwyn was rarely wrong.

"It's dulled now that the ward is back up and it's on the inside, but yes it's magical. And no, it's not the sort of magic that could blow a hole in the wards in case you were wondering."

I had been. Actually, I'd been wondering something else. "The wards cover a huge span. It's too much of a coincidence for this to be in the exact spot where a break was. I'm beginning to think a fairy or a pixie helped Lucien escape and he dropped the coin." Something heavy settled in my chest at the thought. Why had he left? He hadn't seemed all that eager to get out of town at the anger management meeting? Hadn't he trusted me to keep him out of jail?

I thought he'd been sticking around more because of me than that anklet. Maybe I was wrong. Maybe I was just someone to flirt with until he could get the hell out of Accident and back to whatever life he had on the outside. Yes, we Perkins women were definitely cursed when it came to matters of the heart.

"Sheriff is going to be pissed," Bronwyn told me.

"No one is going to care. Marcus said he was dropping the charges. The only issue is we're out an enchanted anklet and there's a newb running around with stories of trolls and cyclops and witches and werewolves."

Bronwyn's lips twitched. "A newb who tells everyone he's the son of Satan. I'm not too worried everyone is going to believe him. And if the guy really is a demon, then he's hardly going to go tattling on us."

I flipped the coin in the air, catching it in my palm. "And

what about this? It's not just some kid's game token from an amusement park according to you. Cursed?"

"Maybe it was cursed to make him think he was a demon, to make him crazy." She grinned at me. "And it doesn't work on you because you're already crazy."

I pocketed the coin and swatted at her. "Brat. Come on. It's Friday night just shy of a full moon and I have half a pint of ice cream waiting for me at home."

CHAPTER 10

CASSANDRA

e were just turning on Main Street when I saw a figure walking down the street—a figure that not only made my heart skip a beat but caused the coin in my pocket to warm to a level that gave me concerns as to the flammability of my silk-poly blend pants. I hoped the damned things didn't catch on fire. Wouldn't that be ironic?

"Pull over! Pull over!" I told Bronwyn. She shot me a perplexed look, then did as I demanded, barely bringing the truck to stop before I was out of it and jogging down the shoulder.

"Hey!" I panted in front of Lucien, not sure what exactly to accuse him of. Seeing the coin and the broken wards, I'd been convinced he'd paid some fairy to get him out of town. Him walking down the street was the last thing I'd expected to see.

"Hey yourself." He grinned. "You here to offer me a ride back to the hotel? Because I won't say 'no' to that. Actually, I won't say 'no' to pretty much anything you'd like to propose."

Good grief, had the almost full moon driven everyone in town sex crazy?

"Why are you here? Where did you go? You were supposed to stay in the hotel." I still hadn't quite caught my breath or my thoughts, and this sexy guy in front of me wasn't making it any easier to think clearly. Maybe I was affected by the moon as well. I heard the slam of a truck door and realized that Bronwyn was making her way over to us, at a much slower pace than I'd done.

Lucien glanced over my shoulder, then back to me, pulling up the hem of his pants to show me the anklet. "This says I can't leave town. Nobody said anything about having to stay in the hotel. What's the use of getting out of jail with a monitoring device if I have to stay locked in a hotel room?"

"Where were you?" I demanded.

He folded his arms across his chest, shooting another quick glance over my shoulder before giving me what he probably thought was a panty-melting smile.

Okay, it was panty melting. And speaking of melting, that coin in my pocket was about ready to burn a hole through the fabric.

"Alberta and John asked me to join them for a happy hour drink." He leaned toward me. "Jealous? Because I would have rather been with you."

"Jealous?" I sputtered. "Of a troll and a cyclops? Please!"

"Hey, is this the hot hellboy?" Bronwyn stepped up beside me and stuck out her hand. "I'm her sister. Bronwyn."

"Lucien. Is she always this grumpy?"

"Yes."

"Traitor," I told Bronwyn before turning back to the demon. "So drinks with Alberta and John where? When did you leave, and did you go anywhere else?"

He regarded me with raised brows. "Lawyers. It's all questions with them. Although I'd thought since you were *my* lawyer, you wouldn't be quite so antagonistic."

"She's antagonistic to everyone," Bronwyn told him. "Don't take it personal."

I eyed him. He was disheveled, as if he'd rolled through a parking lot and a few bushes, but he wasn't quite as mud-covered as Bronwyn was. But then again, if someone had flown him over top of the wards, he wouldn't have had to scramble over a muddy, thorny deadfall.

But then why was he here and not halfway to Boston? Or hell? Or wherever home was? For some reason he'd left town and decided to come back while the wards were down, and had taken a less mud-filled path back than over the deadfall.

Had he forgotten something and needed to return? I felt the coin in my pocket and scowled. It wasn't longing for me that had brought him back to town, it was a missing coin—a coin to call his infernal Uber driver.

"I need to know your exact whereabouts from when we left the meeting until right now."

"Yes sir," he teased. "I went to some watering hole with Alberta and John for a drink. Not the place I was at last night. This was at the other end of town. Red's or something like that."

"Red Brick Tavern," I told him. "How did you pay for a drink when you have no money?"

He wiggled his eyebrows. "Demons don't need money, well unless they're trying to post bail it seems. But I didn't need to stiff the tavern. Alberta paid."

He had a thing for trolls? Alberta did have a sort of earthy appeal to some supernatural beings, especially those who were strong enough not to break in her embrace. Maybe demons enjoyed a night under the bridge with a troll. But he'd not seemed interested that way in Alberta at the meeting. No, he'd seemed interested in *me*. And besides, I knew that Alberta wasn't a quickie kind of woman. If someone joined her under the bridge, they were there until dawn.

"So you had a drink. Then what?" I urged him to continue.

That smirk never left his face. "Then we had a few more. Then I got into a brawl. Then I had a few more drinks. They kicked me out and since the manager had one of those sticks, I decided not to raise a fuss about it. I started heading back to the hotel."

"And Alberta back to her bridge," I finished, trying to figure out if he was telling the truth or not.

Lucien shrugged. "I guess. She left after the fight along with the others."

"Wait, what others? And who were you fighting?"

Still smirking. "I'm a demon, remember? The brawls were with two guys. Not that I'm averse to fighting with a woman, you know. Just so happens mostly men want to throw a punch. Or make me want to throw a punch."

I couldn't argue with that. "Two men? Who?"

"I didn't check their ID or ask their names," he drawled. "First guy said something I didn't appreciate. He ran off after the first punch. Bartender didn't want to let me back in, but Alberta sweet-talked him into letting me stay and got me another drink."

Two fights and a whole lot of booze. That didn't sound like it left much time for him to bribe a fairy into flying him out of town, but fairies could move quick if they were motivated, even carrying a muscled man...or demon. "And the second guy?"

He shuffled his feet and looked down. Was he...embarrassed? A demon was embarrassed?

"Clinton Dickskin," he muttered.

"Who?" I couldn't keep the incredulous tone out of my voice. Bronwyn snickered.

Yes, definitely embarrassed. Lucien shot me a sheepish grin. "It was like something in one of those western movies. Alberta and some woman with Dickskin hustled us both outside. We got into it in the parking lot. I knocked him out, then I went back in for another drink."

I blew a breath out my mouth and ran a hand over my hair. "Damn it, Lucien. I talked to the prosecutor. He was going to talk to Clinton in the morning and have the charges dropped. And now I hear you were fighting with him again and knocked him out? Why couldn't you just stay in the damned hotel for the night?"

"Because that's no fun. How does this law stuff work here in Accident? If I press charges first, does that help? He threw the first punch."

"You knocked him out!" I was actually kind of impressed. Other than some rumpled clothes, Lucien looked fine. No additional bruises or black eyes. He'd fought with a werewolf that was known for not losing in a fistfight, won, and looked as if he'd hardly broken a sweat.

Yeah, this guy was far more sexy than a player panther shifter.

And Lucien seemed to realize that. "Just for a few seconds. He was getting to his feet before I was halfway across the parking lot," He took a step closer. "He deserved it. Punishment. Justice. We're not that different, Cassandra Perkins."

"Except I'm a defense attorney, remember? I'm on the other side of the justice equation."

Bronwyn snorted. "Does that make you an angel, Cassie? That would be a first."

"Two sides of the same coin," Lucien continued. "Angels are about reward. You're not about reward, are you Cassandra?"

Ooo, there was something in his deep voice that made me

want to be allll about reward. Punishment? Yeah, no. That wasn't really my thing. Sylvie had all those books where men tie their women up and do hot sexy-time stuff. Sounded good between the covers of a book. Not so appealing between the covers of a bed, in my opinion.

"I'm about winning. I'm about giving my client a fair shake under the parameters of our legal system. I only play one role in justice. I'm not in charge of delivering it as a social concept beyond that. Knowing I did my best for my client? That's my reward. That and a paycheck." I shot him a steely glare. "But that has nothing to do with you getting into a fight with two more people, when I'm trying to get you off the hook for last night and get you out of town. Why'd you come back, anyway? You were free and clear. We've got no way to track you down, whether you go to hell or not."

He frowned, seeming to be genuinely confused. "What are you talking about?"

"You left town. Paid some fairy to break the wards or fly you over. And I know why you came back too."

Flames leapt deep in his eyes. "If all I had to do to leave this town was fly over your magical wards, then I wouldn't need a fairy to do it."

He stepped back and I heard the sound of ripping fabric. Bronwyn gasped. I was too in shock to do anything but stare. Before me stood Lucien with a tattered shirt, huge black leathery wings extending from his back.

"I don't need a damned fairy to fly anywhere," he snarled.

"I see that." Bronwyn circled around him. "Nice, bro. Diggin the wings there. Horns? Tail? Because I'm thinking you might be hiding the whole package."

He *was* a demon. He was really a demon. I'd begun to suspect he was some sort of supernatural being, and even taken to calling him a demon, but now, with these black wings right in my face, it all hit home.

He was a demon. From hell. In my town.

Lucien stared at me. "You don't want to see my true form. I'm sorry I showed you my wings. I just…"

"You just got angry," Bronwyn finished for him. "Hell, you and Cassie are a match made in heaven. Did you know she set her ex's pants on fire in the middle of the courtroom? Hey, can you do fire as well? Without a spell, I suppose. I mean, it's probably a natural God-given talent. Or Satan-given talent. Sorry."

He continued to stare at me. "I can't do fire inside the town wards. I tried. Evidently I *can* manifest my wings, though. Cassie?"

"Why wouldn't I want to see your true form?" I asked him, feeling myself drawn in by the fire in his eyes.

He grimaced. "It's big. And black."

Bronwyn snorted. "That's what *she* said."

"Wynnie," I warned.

"I'm not as sexy to humans in my demon form," he finished.

I took a breath. "Lucien, I live in a town with minotaur, trolls, cyclops, a medusa… Do you know why Alberta chose to live here in Accident? Trolls have glamour. She could live under any bridge and assume a beautiful form when she wanted to get laid, but here she can be herself. Here no one bats an eye about her appearance. Here someone would fall in love with her as she is—inside and out."

I waited. The wings vanished, leaving me looking at a gorgeous, muscular man with a tattered shirt, one that looked human.

I sighed. Oh well. Wasn't like I'd bared my soul to him either. "So you didn't leave town? Or try to leave town?"

He shook his head. "No. I drank. I fought. I went in and drank some more. Then I started walking back to town and my hotel."

"Then why was this on the other side of the break in the wards?" I pulled the coin out of my pocket and tossed it to him. It flipped end over end, brass glinting in the moonlight.

He caught it midair and looked down at it in his palm.

"Where did you find this?"

"Where you dropped it." I hesitated a moment. "Unless yours is still in your pocket and there's another demon in town who happened to have lost his Uber coin."

He scowled down at the token, then reached in his pocket. "Mine's gone. It must have fell out during one of the fights. That's never happened before. Of course, this whole town has been full of things that have never happened to me before."

"We didn't find it outside the tavern," Bronwyn told him. "So you wanna tell us what you were doing on out on Beaverton Road, half a mile past the turnoff for Meadowland Lane?"

He blinked at her. "I don't even know where that is. What exactly are you both accusing me of? I went to a bar with a cyclops and a troll, had a few drinks, got in a few fights, and eventually started walking back to town. If I dropped the coin, it probably was during one of the fights. So if you didn't find it in the parking lot of the tavern, then obviously someone picked it up only to drop it somewhere else later."

It was a whole lot of coincidence, but I couldn't ignore the fact that he was right here before me, and the only reason he'd have to break the wards would be to leave town. Why break them and stay? It didn't make sense.

"Well, come on then your infernal majesty. We'll give you a lift back to the hotel." Bronwyn gestured toward her truck. "Can't have you walking around with your shirt torn up. Half-naked demon that looks like you would probably drive half the town crazy."

We went back to the truck and I realized our dilemma.

Bronwyn's vehicle had only the front bench-style seat. I couldn't exactly ask him to ride in the back of the bed. First, it would be dangerous. Secondly, it would be illegal. I doubt the first would be much of an issue since I was assuming demons weren't as susceptible to injuries from being tossed out of a moving vehicle as humans were. And normally the second one wouldn't have bothered me, but I figured Lucien had done enough breaking of the law in the last twenty-four hours. No sense in pushing our luck further. Although with my luck, it would probably be Bronwyn and me with the tickets and not him.

Deciding I'd rather be in the middle to safeguard my sister in case this demon got any crazy evil ideas, I climbed in first and scooted over. This way if he did anything horrible, I could kick him out the door. Or set his pants on fire. Either one.

Lucien climbed in, making the truck extra cozy. His leg pressed against mine. His shoulder likewise. And he basically had a choice of putting his arm along the side of my boob with his hand on top of my thigh, or wrap it around my shoulders.

He chose the latter.

It had been a long time since a hot guy had his arm around me. He was warm. He smelled good. And being pressed against him like this was making me imagine how nice it would be to press other parts of my body against his. Naked. In bed.

By the time Bronwyn pulled up to the hotel, I was more than a little hot and bothered. Lucien took his time in the process of exiting the car, doing everything but feeling me up as he shifted around, finally managing to open the passenger side door.

He got out. I got out, intending to escort him to his room, then leave.

Leave. Not stay and have sex with him on that lumpy mattress. Not take him back to my house. Leave.

"Think you should lock him in?" my sister asked me from the truck.

"Huh?" I was too busy wondering how I could get away with sleeping with a client. Was he technically still a client? Marcus did say he intended to drop the charges. Even though the paperwork wasn't done, I might be able to rationalize it all as a done deal.

Bronwyn rolled her eyes, knowing full well where my mind, and my hormones, had gone. Sharing a bedroom with me for my entire childhood meant she knew me far better than any of my other sisters.

"If you're worried about him going out and getting in fights before you can get the charges dropped and him out of town, then maybe he should be on house arrest." Bronwyn nodded toward the door.

"Hey. The only way I'll be on house arrest is if I get to stay at Cassandra's house."

Oh, so tempted. "It's just until morning," I told him. "I promise I'll come get you after breakfast."

"That's not part of the terms of my bail." His eyes glowed that eerie red-orange again. "I agreed to stay in the town until my hearing or until the charges were dropped. Never did I agree to remaining in a hotel room. You'll make a lousy demon, Cassandra, if you can't be specific in your contracts. As a lawyer, I would have thought you would have known that."

"Well for normal folk, the anklet works. Actually, for normal folk we don't even need the anklet." I glared at him. "I'm considering using extraordinary methods because you're not just going out for pizza or getting a beer at a local bar, you're fighting. Again. You're going to end up back in jail. Don't you want to get back home?"

He gave me a slow smile. "No, not really. I'm kind of liking it here. I might stay."

"Well, you don't have any money. And don't you have a job to get back to torturing souls in the third circle?"

"Third, fourth, and sixth," he corrected me. "And demons don't need money. No, I think I'm going to stay. This town is far more interesting than I'd thought. I clearly owe Charon a debt of gratitude when I see him next."

"Well staying here won't be as much fun if you're in jail," I reminded him. "I'm going to lock you in the hotel room and I'll return in the morning to get you."

That glow was back in his eyes. The air felt oddly heavy. We were about to have an argument, and the thought turned me on even more. Yes, psycho me. I had anger management issues, and I got hot and bothered disagreeing with others. Maybe that's why I'd become a lawyer.

"Cassandra Nicole Perkins, the only way you're locking me in that hotel room is if you're on the inside with me."

I sucked in a breath. How the hell had he known my middle name? But that was a minor concern. I was rusty. I wasn't anywhere near as skilled as I'd be if I'd been regularly practicing my witchy arts. Wards aside, I was pretty sure if I went head-to-head with this demon, I was going to lose.

I'd lock him in. He'd walk right out. And I was pretty sure he'd show up at my house just to make sure I knew how ineffective my spell had been. The wards around Accident might have stripped him of most of his demon powers, but I had no doubt that there were a few things beyond sprouting a set of leathery wings that this demon still could do.

"Will you please promise me you'll stay inside the hotel room until I come get you tomorrow?" I had a weird feeling that he'd be good to his word. Maybe there had been something in Grandma's books about demons and making promises, but I was sure I could trust him to do as he said.

Although if demons were like lawyers, he might find some way to wiggle out based on vague contract terms, so I'd need to keep it simple and make sure anything I asked couldn't be interpreted another way.

"Now why would I promise that?" he purred.

Hell if I knew. "Because I asked you to? And said please?" I gave him my best smile, hoping that might help.

"Quid pro quo, darling. It's not a deal unless I get something of equal value in return."

Damn it. "I'll buy you lunch," I offered.

He stepped up to me so close that I could feel the heat of his body against me, feel his breath stir the hair next to my ear. "Fuck me and I'll stay in the room until dawn."

Oh, I so wanted to do just that. But I didn't end up on the review board of my law school for lack of negotiation skills. "Lunch and extra fries. I am representing you pro bono, and I did give you back your coin that you somehow lost. Plus, I gave you a ride back to your hotel."

"Your sister was technically the one who gave me a ride back here. It's her truck, and she's driving."

He never looked at Bronwyn, every ounce of his attention still firmly on me. I was so hot I thought I was about to burst into flames. All of me, not just my pants.

"How about I buy you lunch and I give you a kiss in return for you agreeing to remain in your hotel room until dawn?" I have no idea what made me propose that. Drawing in a shaky breath, I evaluated the state of my willpower and found it sorely lacking. Oh well. I'd need to hold strong and wrench myself away from this guy with only one kiss. Good thing my sister was here watching, as backup in case I started shucking my clothing, or climbing all over this guy.

"You have to walk into the hotel room with me and give me the kiss with the door closed behind you. The kiss, and/or kissing session, cannot be less than thirty seconds long, and there are no restrictions as to what my hands, tongue, or other body parts do during said kiss." His mouth brushed my ear. "And you cook me breakfast in the morning. At your house."

I turned into him, my lips lightly touching his cheek. "I've already got a breakfast date to get Clinton to drop his charges against you. And trust me, babe, you don't want to eat my cooking. Witch. Caldron. Eye of newt."

"Maybe I like eye of newt," he breathed.

"Can I leave? Are you guys going to boink right here on the pavement, or in the hotel? If so, then get it done because I've got a rather impatient centaur that threw a shoe over at the golf course."

"Thirty seconds once I'm inside, Wynnie," I told her. Then I pulled away from the warmth of Lucien's body and boldly walked to his hotel room, unlocking the door with the spare key Hollister had given me when I'd checked my client in, and throwing open the door.

What I saw inside drove all thoughts of sex right out of my mind.

CHAPTER 11

CASSANDRA

"Well, housekeeping services here leave a lot to be desired," Lucien announced cheerfully as he urged me forward into the trashed room.

"What happened?" I stared open-mouthed at the wreckage. The mattress had been slashed, foam and torn springs littering the floor. The mirror was smashed as was the television. All the drawers in the dresser had been pulled out and crushed. The lamp was bent, as if someone had use it to bludgeon a granite statue.

Lucien shrugged. "Party? Hell if I know." He came around the front of me, drawing me into his arms.

I pushed him off. "Did you do this? Was it like this when you left?"

"No. No. I don't care. I've slept in worse. Now about that kiss…"

I held out a hand to stay him and stared at the very wet and very red stain on the carpet. "That's blood."

"Yep. Sure looks like it."

It was a lot of blood. As in, a volume of blood the loss of which would be fatal to a human, and most likely severely debilitating to a supernatural being. Why wasn't Lucien bothered about this? His hotel room was torn to bits, someone had possibly bled out on his floor, and he was acting as though this was not only commonplace, but a non-issue.

Oh. Demon. A dude with leathery wings who made his home in hell and had a job involving torturing and punishing condemned souls wasn't likely to be shocked by what appeared to be a crime scene.

But I was no demon.

I pulled my phone out of my pocket and dialed. "I've got to call this in. If you didn't trash this hotel room, then someone else did. And I'm not feeling like we should ignore the fact that there's a huge blood stain on the rug here."

I dialed the Sherriff's office, not really wanting to call 911 when as far as I could tell there was no one requiring immediate medical attention. Unless…

"Lucien, can you check in the bathroom and on the other side of the beds. Oh, and in the closet? Just in case there's some guy bleeding out still here?"

His lips twitched. I'm glad he found my stoic indifference amusing because most guys didn't. Marcus didn't care as long as I was sleeping with him and giving him all my emotional attention. The fact that I wasn't screaming and shaking over a huge blood stain or panicked over the thought of a possible dead body somewhere in the room was exactly the sort of "emotional distance" that had bothered any human boyfriend I'd ever had.

I chalked it up to being raised in a town full of supernatural beings for whom "bleeding out" wasn't necessarily fatal, and most of whom would have been making jokes right now.

"No dead guy. Or injured guy," Lucien cheerfully informed me. "Now get off the phone so I can have my kiss. Although I'm not relishing the thought of spending the night in this mess. Perhaps I should take this as an occasion to renegotiate our deal."

"I'm not spending the night with you," I told him before turning my attention back to the phone. "No, not you Fred. I was talking to someone else. Yes, Hollister's Hotel. Room six. No, I haven't identified what kind of blood it is."

I hung up, then dialed the one person who *could* identify what sort of being this stain had belonged to. Yes, I could do it, but it would take a whole lot of components that I didn't carry around on me. And I didn't practice magic. Unless I could help it anyway.

"Ophelia? Can you come over to the hotel, room six?"

My sister sighed. "Should I bring my medical bag? Did you knife someone, Cassie? What did this one do, pull your braids in first grade or something?"

Did I mention my sister was a paramedic, probably trying to catch a few winks on a cot at the firehouse between calls? You'd think a town full of supernaturals wouldn't require much in the way of emergency medical help, but we were just a day away from the full moon, and things did get rather messy around here at that time of the month.

"I just need a quick divination," I told her.

"You do know I'm on tonight, right?"

"Quick, I promise. There's a blood stain on the carpet here and I need to know who might be dead."

She sighed and I heard a noise as if she were putting her pants on. "If I'm lucky I can tell you 'what'. The 'who' is beyond my ability."

"I'll take it." I hung up just as Sheriff Oakes came through the door, followed by Bronwyn.

"Christ, Cassie. I figured you'd just decided to screw the guy, but then the cops show up and I'm worried that maybe you set his pants on fire. Or set something else on fire."

"We screw and this whole hotel is burning down, I promise you that," Lucien told her with a grin.

"Out," Oakes instructed us all. "Not you," he told Lucien.

"I'm his attorney." Which meant I got to stay as well.

The sheriff shook his head. "Fine. First off, where was your client while this was going on?"

"I don't exactly know when this happened," Lucien told him. "I was with Cassie at an anger management meeting, then went with a cyclops and a troll to have a few beers. I've got witnesses. Or is it an alibi? What do you all call it?"

I shushed him. "My client can prove where he was all night. This probably had nothing to do with him. Someone got the wrong room number, and trashed the place, upset because they couldn't find whatever it was they were trying to steal."

"And stubbed their toe on the bedframe on the way out?" Fred scoffed. "Because that's a lot of blood, Cassie."

"Lucien was walking along the street alone when we picked him up," Bronwyn added unhelpfully. "I'm sure there's a gap between when everyone last saw him at the tavern and we saw him on the road. He's a demon. Maybe he runs really fast or teleports." She snapped her fingers. "Or flies. He's got wings. I'll bet he flew here, saw someone robbing the place and stabbed him a few times with demon claws, then flew back to make it look like he was just leaving the tavern."

"Not helping," I snapped at her.

Bronwyn had a fantastic imagination. I glared at her and turned back to the sheriff.

"My client is wearing the same clothes as when I saw him last. He doesn't have anything else to wear. If he'd done this, he would be covered in blood. And he would have had no reason to be flying around, stabbing people with...alleged demon claws."

"I do have demon claws," Lucien announced.

"Not helping," I retorted. What was with these people? Everyone needed to be quiet and let me be a lawyer here.

"Paramedic, divination witch, and occasional CSI coming through." My sister Ophelia pushed her way past Bronwyn and stared matter-of-factly down at the blood stain. She and Sylvie were the twins of our family. They were equally tall, equally thin, equally dark-haired with somewhat pointed noises and definitely pointed chins. But where Sylvie was a gym-rat health nut, Ophelia looked as if she'd spent most of her life sequestered in a coffin with a vampire sucking her blood. She wasn't Goth, she just naturally looked Goth.

I grabbed Lucien's sleeve and pulled him aside as the other two took a step away from the crimson stain. Ophelia pulled a series of stones out of her bag, carefully arranging them around the edge of the blood-soaked section of carpet.

"Lotta blood," she muttered. "Whole lotta of blood."

"Is that the incantation?" Lucien whispered.

"No, she just likes to talk to herself as she casts," I whispered back.

Once the stones were arranged to her liking, Ophelia pulled little twigs of dried herbs from her other pocket, putting them at key spots. Then she pulled out a Bic lighter.

"Hollister's gonna kill you for burning holes in his carpet," I warned her.

"He's gonna have to replace it anyway with this big red spot," she replied.

"Nah, he'll just slap some bleach over it and move the bed over a few feet to cover it up," Bronwyn said. "Burn away, sis."

Eww. But she wasn't wrong. Hollister wasn't exactly known for running a five-star hotel, and with a wedding this weekend, he wouldn't have time to replace the carpet. No way he'd lose out on a room rental just because of a huge blood stain and some burn marks. That's why God invented bleach and Febreze, you know.

The herbs smoldered, sending the aroma of rosemary and burnt carpet fibers into the air.

"You know we're all going to get cancer from this," Bronwyn told her.

"Glenda will heal us," Ophelia said. "Now hush. I've got to concentrate."

The sheriff took a step toward the door and gestured for Lucien to follow. "I'm going outside. You might want to as well, buddy. Witch magic feels like someone poured itching powder down your underwear."

Lucien's eyebrows shot up. "I'll take my chances." The demon did move closer to the door, though, clearly not as willing to have his nether regions itchy as he claimed.

Ophelia took a breath and began to chant. Unlike Sheriff Oakes had claimed, the magic wasn't itchy, or unpleasant—at least not to me. Goosebumps raised on my skin as my sister's spell shivered over me like a ghostly hand. My own magic rose from deep inside me, eager to answer the call. I pushed it down firmly, and glanced over to see Bronwyn, her eyes glowing electric blue, white light like a fog curling from her fingertips. Lucien watched, transfixed. As he looked at me, I saw the lust in his eyes. He was turned on. Our magic didn't frighten him or make him feel like he was itching. It wasn't unpleasant to him, it was an aphrodisiac.

The thought shredded my control and I let my magic fly, feeling it surge out through my skin, giving power to Ophelia's spell.

My skin tingled when it was done. I felt more alive than I had in years. And I was scared. If I gave in to magic, if I allowed myself to accept my witch gifts, then I also needed to accept the destiny of my birth. No. I didn't want responsibility for this town and its residents. No, I didn't want to be the one everyone came to when there was a problem. I just wanted to be Cassie Perkins, that lawyer who lived up on the hill in her family's old home. Just a normal citizen—well, as normal as any of us were in this town.

"Werewolf," Ophelia said as she dusted off her hands and gathered up the stones.

"So someone slaughtered a werewolf in this hotel room," the sheriff said from outside the doorway.

"No, someone smeared a bunch of werewolf blood in the carpet of this hotel room." Ophelia shot the man a wry grin. "I don't need to be a witch to know that. Look at the edges. And there's no spray, no other blood besides this spot. Shot, stabbed, or whatever, the victim would have decorated the bed and possibly the walls with droplets and streaks of blood. They would have clutched at the wound, leaving a hand print as they slid to the floor. And they would have left a dragged trail of blood as their body was removed."

The sheriff nodded then shot her an embarrassed look. "I don't get many murder scenes here, you know. Mostly theft. Or people beating up other people, usually because someone stole something. Last time I seen this much blood was when that minotaur gored the ogre in that bar fight. Or butchering day over at Sally Chesterfield's."

"So someone wanted us to think a werewolf was stabbed, or maybe even killed, here," I mused. "Which means they probably wanted to frame Lucien for the supposed crime."

"Well, I have established a bit of a pattern when it comes to fighting with shifters," Lucien chimed in. "I guess it's not too far of a stretch to think I might have killed one."

"But why?" Bronwyn asked. "Lucien's only been in town, what? Just over twenty-four hours? It's not long enough for someone to have a feud going with him."

"Besides Clinton Dickskin," I reminded her. "And maybe whatever other shifter Lucien has been fighting." I frowned, going through our shifter population in my head. Clinton. Stanley, although he wouldn't do anything without Clinton's approval. Then that other guy Lucien had fought tonight...

"Wait, the other guy your fought was a shifter? What kind of shifter?"

Lucien's expression turned wary. "I'm not sure," he lied.

I knew he lied. I could feel it in my very bones. "But you knew he was a shifter, so either you saw him shift, or there's something about you that allows you to recognize them, or someone identified him for you." I scowled. "Which was it?"

He shrugged. "Alberta said he was a shifter. I only knew he was an asshole and deserved my fist in his face."

"A panther shifter, I'm guessing?"

He grinned. "Good guess. You can take the demon out of hell, but you can't change his nature. I punish. I seek justice. It's what I do. Kind of hard for me to let that go."

I rolled my eyes. "Next time make a citizen's arrest, or call 911. Lucien, you've got to stop getting in fights or you'll never get out of this town."

"I'm thinking of extending my vacation anyway," he said with a slow smile. "Things here in Accident are far more interesting than I'd ever suspected."

"Flirt later," Bronwyn told him. "We've got a possible crime scene here, and a sheriff that could really use our help."

The sheriff nodded gratefully. "So as far as people who may have wanted to frame you for something, we've got Clinton Dickskin, and there's only one panther shifter in town. I'll question them both, because I know better than to send Cassie over to talk to Marcus."

"Hey," I protested. "I just spoke to him this evening and managed to not incinerate anything. Think I can control myself. I can tell you right now that this isn't Marcus' style. He'd sue, or key your car or something, but not risk staining his nice clothes by transporting blood and smearing it around on a carpet."

"Well it's *not* Clinton Dickskin who did this. I'm pretty sure of that," Ophelia commented drily. "Because this divination came through clear as can be. It's not just any old werewolf blood on the carpet, it's Clinton Dickskin's blood."

I caught my breath. That meant someone had either killed or severely wounded Clinton, and knew enough about Lucien's two run-ins with the werewolf to attempt to frame him for the crime.

The fight last night outside a crowded Pistol Pete's. Everyone at the courthouse, at the anger management meeting. Everyone who was at the Red Brick Tavern and saw Lucien's second fight with the werewolf. Pretty much everyone in town knew the demon and the werewolf had exchanged blows at least once.

So the question wasn't who knew enough to frame Lucien, it was who wanted Clinton Dickskin dead. And unfortunately the answer to that question was the same as the first one—pretty much everyone in town.

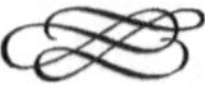

CHAPTER 12

*B*ronwyn dropped us off at a house that looked like it had been cobbled together over the centuries, then sped off to take care of some centaur's lost horseshoe. Or whatever. Cassie stood in front of the door, suddenly nervous.

"I won't hurt you, you know," I told her. "I can't seem to do much in this town besides beat up werewolves."

"If you can beat up a werewolf, you can easily overpower me," she countered.

"You're a witch," I told her. "You can easily overpower me."

"I don't know if you understand how uncomfortable I am with allowing a man I've known less than twelve hours, a demon no less, spend the night in my house—my *family* house, the one I grew up in."

I didn't understand that. And I was sure she didn't understand how much power she held in this thing between us. Even if I hadn't been hampered by the town's wards, a powerful witch had the ability to banish, to command, and control. Maybe it was just as well she didn't realize that, because I was looking for a partnership, not servitude. Sometimes a demon got on the wrong side of a contract. Sometimes there was nothing he could do to prevent that from happening.

Maybe I didn't quite trust her either.

"This was your grandmother's house?"

Cassie nodded. "Generations of Perkins witches have lived here. I grew up here with my grandmother and my mother. When Grandma died and Mom lit out...well, this is where I stayed with my sisters. It's where I raised them."

That's when it hit me—for nearly a decade, it had always been just Cassie. She'd been a teenager, and suddenly she was in charge of six younger siblings, the eldest witch in a town. No wonder she had anger issues. No wonder she didn't want any further responsibility on her shoulders.

She reached out for the doorknob, that little frown still creasing her brow.

I put a hand on her shoulder. "I promise you that I won't harm you. As long as I'm in your house, I'll abide by your rules and do whatever you say. Demons don't break promises."

I shivered a bit at that, knowing that I had just put myself in her hands—at least while I was under this roof. Although if she forbade me to leave the house, I'd really be in trouble.

Idiot. These are the sorts of fools' bargains demons agree to when they're thinking with their libido.

"You don't enter my room unless asked." She blushed a bit at the "asked" part, as if she were thinking of doing just that. "No removing anything from the house—spell books, wands or broomsticks, the good china..."

What in the hell would I do with good china? Or any china? "Agreed."

"And no trashing the place, or smearing werewolf blood on the carpet," she added with a quick smile.

"Agreed. You believe I'm innocent of that, right?" I asked.

She opened the door. "Oh, I believe you're anything but innocent. But I'm sure that if you'd decided to off Clinton Dickskin, you wouldn't frame yourself by rubbing blood on the carpet of your own hotel room, then inviting me in for a make-out session."

"They'll probably find him sleeping off a fifth of whisky in a ditch somewhere with an IV in his arm," I conjectured.

She flicked on the lights and stepped inside. "It takes more than a fifth of whisky to get a werewolf drunk, especially this close to the full moon."

"Nice house." I stood in the doorway, admiring the décor. Where the outside was clearly a series of additions onto an original small home, the inside was seamlessly spacious. Open but cozy with bright splashes of color on pillowy couches and fleecy throws.

"So are you demons like vampires or something? Do I need to invite you in?"

I grinned and stepped across the threshold. "No. Just being polite. You'll be relieved to know that we demons can come and go pretty much anywhere we like—your houses, your places of worship."

"Possess our bodies?" she teased, tossing her car keys on a table.

"There's only one body I'm thinking of possessing right now." I took a step toward her, hesitating when she took one back in response. "But it's been a long day. I'm sure you're tired. Where am I sleeping if it's not in your room?"

"Uh, you can sleep in Adrienne's old room. That's the nice thing about these old houses. They've got lots of bedrooms. Not many bathrooms though. I'm…well, I've got a bit of research to do before I hit the sack. You can sleep. Or help yourself to anything in the kitchen. There's not much in the fridge, I'll warn you. Or television. Or books.

But not the spell books. Do demons know how to read spell books?"

She was rambling, nervous, and I wasn't sure what to do to get back to that friendly banter we'd had earlier.

"We can't cast spells, but we can lend our power to witches as they cast spells. Like what you did with your sister in the hotel room when she did her divination? It's the same, only more. With my help, your spells will be more powerful." I eyed the books on the shelf. Most of them were mysteries and romance novels with a few biographies. "What sort of research are you going to do? Demons are also very helpful in information gathering and research. That's one of the main reasons witches summon us."

She tilted her head, relaxing noticeably. "I've never known witches to summon demons. How does that work, exactly? Does it piss you guys off when that happens? I'd be furious if I was in the middle of a hot shower and bam, I'm all naked and sudsy in front of twelve witches."

I laughed. "I'd pay good money to see that. Yes, sometimes the summoning is inconvenient, but it's usually welcome. We make a big fuss about it all, threatening stuff and telling the coven we're not going to help them, but in reality, partnering with a coven on a spell or sharing information with them is a rush. Partnering with a single witch long term? That's something every demon dreams of. Especially if that partnership carries an emotional and physical bond. But the burning times came close to killing all the witches off. Few remain, and those that do don't summon demons."

"I didn't summon you." Her voice was soft, her gaze tentative as she lifted those dark brown eyes to meet mine.

"No, but I would welcome a partnership with you, Cassandra Nicole Perkins." It felt like equivalent of a marriage proposal. In a way, I guess it was.

"Because I'm a witch and there aren't many of us left?"

"Because you're smart, funny, powerful, and beautiful. Because as ancient as I am, I know that the pair of us together would be an amazing thing. Because I can't think of a better way to spend eternity than by your side."

She bit her lip. "I just met you."

I held very still, afraid that if I moved toward her, I'd ruin whatever tentative thing there was between us. "For a demon, I'm amazingly patient. Take your time, Cassie. I'll wait for you to decide."

"And if I'm eighty when I finally decide?" That teasing smile curled up the corner of her lips.

"Then I'll be partnering with an eighty-year-old witch, and loving every minute of it."

She laughed, then pointed up the stairs. "I was going to do research on demons and witches, but I also wanted to find out some history on the werewolves in Accident. Bronwyn mentioned that there's some unrest—well, more unrest than usual. If there's going to be another alpha war, then I'd like to see how Grandma handled the last one in the sixties. From her journals."

"Well, I can't help with that, but I can see what you've got in your kitchen and make us a late-night snack while you read."

Any remaining nervousness vanished at my words. "Good luck with that. I'll be up in the attic—there's a ladder through the back bedroom upstairs. Come on up with whatever moldy crackers and expired milk you manage to find."

I quickly discovered that she wasn't kidding about the food. There was a nearly empty container of ice cream that looked as if it had thawed and been refrozen. Canned goods. Some pasta and rice in a cupboard. I wasn't all that skilled at cooking, but I managed to whip together a decent pasta primavera with canned veggies and the last of the milk. What I did find was a wine rack filled with bottles. Grabbing a red blend and a couple of glasses, I balanced it all in my arms and headed upstairs, managing to not drop anything as I climbed the ladder to the attic.

Cassie was cross-legged on the floor of the attic, her auburn hair twisted up into a messy bun on top of her head. There was a journal open on her lap, full of cursive writing.

She glanced up at me with a smile. "Smells good, whatever it is."

"Pasta." I sat the bowl down and handed her a fork before dropping to sit next to her. "Hope you drink your coffee black because I used the last of the milk."

"There's some non-dairy stuff somewhere." She dug into the pasta while I opened the wine. "Yum. This is pretty good for cobbled-together late-night dinner. These canned peas?"

"No, I quickly grew some in a garden out back," I teased. "Of course they're canned. Don't you have any fresh fruit or vegetables in this house at all?"

"I buy them, and by the time I go to eat them they're rotted. So why bother?" She took the glass of wine I handed her and sipped it. Looking back down at the journal. "This is…well, kind of hard to read. You get a certain idea in your head about your parents and grandparents, then find out they weren't quite who you thought they were. It's strange."

"So Grandma was a swinger? Snorted coke and had orgies with vampires in the back bedroom while you all were asleep? That sort of thing?"

She shot me an odd look. "Uh, no. I always thought she was this powerful witch, and here she's worrying about the werewolves and the violence up on the mountain, worried that she can't control them or contain it if they start bringing that violence into the town itself. She was struggling just to hold everything together. All by herself. Mom wasn't at all a powerful witch. I'd always thought she was just a loser who bailed on us when Grandma died because she didn't want the responsibility, but reading this…I think she was afraid. I think without Grandma here, she was worried she couldn't manage things on her own."

"That's a lousy excuse for abandoning seven kids," I told her.

Cassie shrugged. "You're right. But it's still a side of her I never considered."

"You've got power." I tapped her wine glass with mine. "I can see it, feel it. You've got the strength to safeguard the town, to keep the werewolves in line. Especially with me by your side."

She snorted. "And if you decide not to stick around?"

"First, I've already made the offer and I'm not backing out on that. You say the word, and I'm here, with you, for as long as you want. Second, you can absolutely hold your own against those werewolves without my help. It won't be easy or painless, but you can do it. Don't doubt yourself. I didn't know your grandmother, but if she had anywhere near your power, she wouldn't have been having issues with the wolves on the mountain."

"Not sure I believe you on that one, but we'll have to agree to disagree." She flipped a page and pointed down at the swirled writing. "This is what really bothers me. Grandma didn't like that the werewolves were able to live under pack law and not the laws of our town, but she didn't feel strong enough to push the issue. The alpha battles…she said in here that some of them weren't legitimate."

"That they were using the excuse of alpha challenges to cover up illegal murders?"

Cassie nodded. "That what should have just been a fight to first blood was taken too far and a wolf killed more for political reasons than because they wouldn't yield. That there might have been cases where a death was covered up as you said. This one…the challenger was a twelve-year-old boy.

Who the hell accepts a challenge from a twelve-year-old boy? Then excuses his death as justifiable under pack law?"

I leaned over her shoulder. "Did your grandmother investigate the death?"

She shook her head, her hair brushing against my cheek. "She tried, but the wolves would only give her the basic information. They claimed pack law. Jurisdiction. It's bullshit, Lucien. Twelve years old."

"And you're worried that might happen again?"

She closed the journal and set it aside. "Yeah. Bronwyn's worried too. I think…I think if I want to keep the peace for the residents here in Accident, that I'm going to have to intervene. Sherriff Oakes is a skilled, dedicated man…or dryad, but there's only so much he can do. The town needs a witch. And out of all my sisters, I'm the one best suited to do this."

There was a note of frustration in her voice. I smoothed a stray lock of her hair to the side, my fingers brushing against her neck. "You're not alone, you know. This isn't like when your mother left and you had to raise six of your sisters. You're not alone."

She turned, her mouth inches from mine. "I know. You offered. And trust me, I'm tempted to take you up on that offer."

I was tempted to do a whole lot more, but not now—not unless she made the first move. "Not just me. You've got six sisters who are ready to back you up with their magic. You've got a dryad sheriff, that rat-shifter of a policeman, trolls and cyclops, and fairies, and whatever else this town has. Every one of them has an interest in keeping this town a peaceful place for them all to live without fear. You're not alone, Cassie."

She leaned forward and touched her lips to mine. Tentative. Soft. Gentle. I held back, letting her take this where she wanted. Slowly she eased back, her eyes raising to meet mine.

"Maybe you shouldn't sleep in Adrienne's bedroom after all."

"Where should I sleep then?" I murmured. "The couch? Here in the attic? Some doghouse out back."

"My room."

She leaned forward again and this kiss had all the runaway passion she'd held back from the previous one. Her tongue tasted mine, her hands bunching up the bottom of my shirt to feel their way up my skin. I dug my fingers into her hair and pulled her to me. She made an impatient noise, shifting to straddle me, pushing me backward onto the ground right into the bowl of pasta.

"Shit! I'm so sorry." She laughed, trying to wipe the food from my shoulder, smearing noodles and peas in cream sauce all across my shirt.

Sitting up, I yanked the shirt over my head, tossing it to the side. She took the opportunity to do the same, revealing a lacy red bra.

"That needs to go as well," I told her.

She hesitated. I took a chance and reached out to trace the edge of the lace with my finger.

"Or not. Your call, sweetheart. Everything we do or don't do is entirely up to you."

She took a breath, then smiled, slowly unhooking the bra, sliding it down from her shoulders and off to join her shirt on the attic floor. With a graceful move she stood, slowly unzipping the skirt and dropping it to the floor. Then she hooked her thumbs in the red panties and shimmied them down to join the skirt.

I stared, drinking in the view. I'd been imagining her naked since I'd first seen her from my jail cell, and my imagination hadn't been anywhere near as spectacular as reality.

"Your turn, hellboy," she teased, her voice husky.

I stood, shucking my pants with far less grace than she'd just done.

"All the way," she said, waving a finger at the underwear that wasn't doing much at hiding my desire.

I complied and she stepped forward, sliding a hand up my chest and around my neck to pull my mouth to hers. She tasted of honey and cinnamon and wine. Her lips and tongue, her body pressed against mine, the thought of her underneath me was almost more than I could stand.

Then she pulled back and I stifled a groan, torn between the desire to take her here and now on this attic floor and to let her move this at her own pace.

It seemed like forever I waited for some sort of signal from her. Finally she tilted her head and shot me a crooked smile. "Let's go downstairs. To my room where we don't have to deal with hard attic floors or spilled bowls of pasta or knocking over the wine."

"Deal," I told her, scooping her into my arms.

We somehow made it downstairs and into her bedroom, kissing all through the hallway like crazed teenagers. And once that witch got me into her bed, that's where I stayed. All night long.

CHAPTER 13

CASSANDRA

I awoke alone in my bed to the smell of bacon and coffee.

Last night…oh wow, last night. My hand crept between my legs as I remembered all the things Lucien and I had done. His tongue working its way up my thighs. His hard length driving deep inside me as I dug my nails into his fine ass. I hadn't gotten much sleep at all, and I was looking forward to more. I hoped this demon stuck around, because a girl could get used to sex like this.

For the first time in a very long time, I felt as if life were truly good—cool clean cotton sheets, soft feather pillows, a warm down comforter. A sexy man who'd rocked my world all night long. He seriously needed to get that cute ass of his up here again so we could snuggle and more. And while he was getting up here, he should also bring some coffee and bacon to me in bed.

I was tempted to slide out from under my sheets and head into the kitchen wearing the tank top and underwear I'd gone to bed in, grab said coffee and bacon, grab the hot guy cooking it all, and take everything back to bed to enjoy properly, but the sound of multiple voices coming from downstairs ended that little fantasy.

Hopping out of bed, I did the morning bathroom essentials, threw on a pair of jeans and a t-shirt, then headed down. In the kitchen I found Lucien along with my sister Glenda. Glenda was at the stove, her personal domain, cooking what looked to be a frittata along with French toast and the bacon I'd smelled from upstairs.

And clearly she'd brought her own supplies, since the only thing in my refrigerator as of last night was a half-empty container of ice cream and some moldy cheese.

"...non GMO, free range, and cage free. That's important, you know. Beyond the ethics of treating other creatures in the most humane way possible, you can taste it in the eggs. Those poor things stacked on top of each other in tiny wire cages, their feet cut from the wires, poop falling down through to each chicken below it...those eggs taste of desperation and pain."

"Lovely visual," I announced. "Not thinking I've got the stomach for breakfast after hearing about chickens pooping down on each other."

Glenda spun around with a smile that never failed to light up my world. "Nothing puts you off your breakfast, Cassie darling. Nothing." She leaned over to give me a smooch on the cheek, then went back to the frittata and her lecture on the ethics of food-chain management. That was Glenda. She was smack in the middle of our line of siblings. Me, Bronwyn, then the twins Ophelia and Sylvie, then Glenda. Only Adrienne and Babylon were younger, but sometimes this quirky sister of mine seemed the eldest of us all. She'd been the one who'd deciphered the bookshelf full of cookbooks and kept us from living on instant oatmeal and frozen pizza once Mom had hit the road. I'd always thought she'd become a chef, but each year her food mantra got more and more dogmatic. Paleo. Keto. Whole Foods. Nothing that wasn't strictly organic, grass-fed, locally sourced. Now she was making noises about veganism, although from the bacon and frittata on the stove, that seemed to still be in the "just talking" phase. Soon I expected her to be trying to convince us all that we needed to only eat seaweed and dandelion roots, or something like that.

Glenda healed. That was her specialty. And in keeping with her quirky nature, she only healed through her food. I was pretty sure that after eating this frittata, the blister on my heel from those new pumps would completely be gone, as well as the paper cut I'd gotten yesterday. Sadly she'd never cured cancer or anything life-threatening, but any time someone had a urinary tract infection, strep throat, or a bad case of athlete's foot, they knew to call on Glenda.

"Morning, sunshine." Lucien poured a cup of coffee, stirred in two spoonfuls of sugar, and handed it to me with a kiss on the top of my head.

Glenda shot me a perceptive side-eye. "So I come by to find this hottie half-naked in the kitchen about to open a can of beans for breakfast. Anything you want to tell me, Cassie?"

"Nope." I sipped my coffee, marveling that Lucien somehow knew exactly how I liked my morning beverage. Was he a mind reader?

"I'm a client," Lucien offered. "Although I'm hoping to become more than a client."

"Well, this coffee is improving your chances," I teased. "Any news on our favorite werewolf this morning? You're not in jail, so I'm taking that as a positive sign. What's your demon intuition tell you?"

"It's telling me I have better things to do on a Saturday morning than worry about a werewolf." He pulled me close, his arm around my shoulder.

"Ophelia texted me about what happened," Glenda

commented, eyeing us with a smirk. "She was on-call at the firehouse. Last thing either of us heard, Clinton Dickskin didn't make it back to his den last night."

I shrugged, but my stomach dropped a few feet at her words. "Full moon is tonight. Not surprising that a werewolf wouldn't come home with their blood stirred up."

"Clinton is an idiot, but not a suicidal one." Glenda flipped the bacon and picked up the pan to gently slide the frittata out onto a plate. "A werewolf loses that much blood, he's not going to continue looking for fights, sex, or any other shenanigans. He would have gone somewhere safe to heal. He would have wanted to make sure he wasn't going into the full moon suffering blood loss and who knows what else."

I frowned, thinking about what I knew about were-wolves, which was a bit more than I knew about demons. "They go all out during the full moon, though. Run until they die. Bleed until they die. They've got no sense of self-preservation or restraint then. One day shouldn't make such a huge difference in that. I mean, the shifters are already feeling the moon a few days before the actual event."

Glenda nodded. "Yeah, but hyped up isn't the same as moon-crazy, and Clinton isn't some random pack member. He's dominant in the pack. A wolf doesn't get that way without knowing when to fold his hand and go home for the evening."

I'd never experienced any of this with Marcus. Feline shifters didn't have packs, and their behavior during the full moon wasn't quite as crazy as the wolves.

"Your sister Ophelia said it was a lot of blood, even for a werewolf," Lucien chimed in. "Maybe he was too weak to make it home. Maybe he was worried that whoever attacked him would be waiting for him to finish the job. If that's the case, he could have decided to bed down in someone's barn or garage, or old shed."

I watched Glenda put the food on the table and debated my conflicting desires to go eat, and to remain here with Lucien's arm around me. He decided for me, sliding his hand from my shoulder down to my ass and urging me toward the table. I sat, waiting for the other two before I snatched up a piece of bacon.

"If Clinton doesn't turn up this morning, we'll need to go search for him. Not that I think he's going to stagger into the Stagecoach for our breakfast meeting after losing all that blood."

"I don't know," Glenda commented. "Their pancakes are pretty good. I might just rise out of my deathbed for a short stack of pecan oat with warm maple syrup."

True. Their pancakes really were that good. "Well, I'm assuming he's not going to be there. Ophelia said he wasn't attacked in the hotel room—that was a manufactured crime scene to set Lucien up for some reason we've yet to determine. If the werewolf is alive and he did decide to spend the night somewhere other than his home, then we'll need to find where he was attacked and search in a radius from there. With that much blood loss, he can't have gone far."

"Unless he had help." Lucien slid a pie-shaped slice of the frittata onto my plate. "A few of those other werewolves were with him after our fight last night. His buddies, I assume. Maybe he got into another fight with someone who was using claws or a knife, and his buddies gave him a lift."

"Then he would have been home." I took a bite of the frittata, marveling as I always did at Glenda's amazing culinary skills. "Unless he told his buddies not to take him home. Who would be pissed enough at Clinton Dickskin that they'd kill him? Or nearly kill him?"

"That much blood loss, I'd normally say vampires,"

Glenda added thoughtfully. "Except they wouldn't waste it dumping the blood in a hotel room."

"This wasn't a vampire getting carried away," I told her. "This was someone who wanted Clinton dead, whether they succeeded or not. They tried to frame Lucien for it. No one is going to do that for a simple brawl where the next morning Clinton can name his attacker. The blood in that hotel room means someone wanted Clinton dead."

"If they killed him, why not leave his body in my hotel room with the blood?" Lucien asked. "It's what I would have done."

He was right. If there had been a dead werewolf in that room, Lucien would be in lockup right now. "Maybe that's what they planned, but Clinton got away and this was the next best thing? Maybe they're hoping he died in a ditch somewhere, and Lucien is still the top suspect?"

"Let's think this through," Lucien said. "I fight with Clinton outside the tavern. His friends haul him off to nurse his bruised ego. Something happens and he either gets into another fight, or someone takes the opportunity to knife him."

I shrugged. "Could be a planned hit and Clinton spoiled it all by managing to get away before dying. Could be a spur-of-the moment thing, and someone frantically tries to pin the blame on you in case Clinton ends up found dead in a ditch the next day. Who knows?"

"Full moon tonight though." Lucien took a bite of his bacon. "Can't be a coincidence."

I nodded. "It's when all the shifters go a bit nuts. The wards help keep the moon sickness somewhat under control, but there's always fights, vandalism, unexpected pregnancies." I remembered the tension between the two werewolves yesterday afternoon, when I'd been at the pack-house asking for the charges against Lucien to be dropped.

"Maybe this is less about the moon, and more about pack politics?" I mused.

Glenda's fork stopped halfway to her mouth. "Crap. Not another alpha fight. That last one nearly destroyed the town."

Not that any of us had been alive for the last one, but that sort of turmoil lived on in legends. Grandma had let the werewolves work it out mostly on their own, only intervening when the violence began to spill over to the rest of the town residents, but even so there had been some property damage, a few broken bones, and no one had felt easy watching the werewolves battle it out on the mountain, or whenever they happened to come to town which had been more frequently than anyone had wanted. In the end, eight werewolves were dead, and Dallas Dickskin had become the new pack alpha. The werewolves still continued to cause trouble, but nothing compared to the battle of the alphas.

"So Clinton makes a play for alpha?" I shook my head. "Not the smartest move after getting beaten up by a demon. You'd think the guy would have the brains to wait until he was fully healed."

"Night before the full moon," Glenda pointed out. "Clinton comes home pissed off. Dallas says the wrong thing. A fight turns into something a whole lot more, and suddenly there's a challenge. Not like those things don't happen all the time in pack hierarchy. Dallas has been riding his ass since Clinton was a teen. If you haven't seen that coming to a head, then you're blind."

There had been a lot of jockeying for position among the werewolves in the last few decades. Heck, last year one of the females nearly unseated Clinton for pack second. The only reason she wasn't dead was because werewolves, especially misogynistic ones like Dallas and Clinton, were reluctant to kill their females.

"But why smear a bunch of blood in my hotel room if

that's the case?" Lucien asked. "Aren't alpha battles exempt from your town laws regarding assault and murder?"

I grimaced. "Sort of. Last time there was an alpha battle was forty years ago. Grandmother allowed the deaths to be considered an internal pack matter as long as no non-werewolf died during the fighting, and as long as the werewolves could show that the challenge battles followed their pack laws and those who died were truly killed in a challenge fight."

"But do you really believe that?" Lucien asked softly.

I met his gaze, knowing what he meant. The diary last night... Grandma had her doubts, but hadn't wanted to go up against a pack of werewolves with only my mother to back, or not back, her up.

"No, but what could one witch do?" I shrugged. "I remember hearing her and Mom discussing it once. I think it had been less of a rules-based challenge battle and more of a gang war up there on the mountain. I think Grandma had her hands full just making sure the violence was contained to the werewolf territories."

But that child... Lucien was clearly remembering that as well.

Glenda pushed her plate away from her. "What would happen if there were an alpha battle now? We've got a mayor and a sheriff, but no Grandma to keep the werewolves in line."

Oh no. I knew where she was going with this. "The mayor and the sheriff are perfectly capable of keeping law and order here. The days of a witch running this town are over."

"Are they?" Lucien sat back in his chair. "Are fights to the death among the werewolves going to be written off as pack politics like they were forty years ago? Are the mayor and sheriff just going to take the alpha's word for it that the dead wolves are challengers who knew this was a fight to the death? Are they capable of making sure the town isn't destroyed by rival werewolf gangs?"

"Sheriff Oakes can handle it," I told him, not believing that for one second. That werewolf child… He'd not been a challenger, and even if he had, a child's life should never have been forfeited in a challenge battle. It was against pack law. It was against human law.

It was against witch law. And as powerful as Grandma had been, she hadn't done anything to stop it. All she could do was turn her head and go to her grave with that child's death on her conscience.

"There are seven of us, Cassie," Glenda said softly. "It doesn't have to be you. It doesn't always have to be you."

But it did, didn't it? My six sisters were powerful witches, but all specialized. I was the only one who wouldn't be limited in what I could do. And of them all, I was the only one who had the sort of power to take control of this town. But why did I have to? Why did a stupid accident of birth mean I had to spend my life dealing with werewolves and the issues of the town?

Damn it all. Everyone in my family knew I wasn't going to just sit back and watch this town get steamrollered by a bunch of fighting werewolves. And everyone knew I wouldn't brush off werewolf deaths without some sort of intense investigation.

The big question was did I have the power to make law and order, and punishment, stick?

I pushed my chair out from the table. "Guess if I'm going to face down Dallas Dickskin and demand to know where he dumped Clinton's body, I better get going. You stay here," I told Lucien as he also got to his feet.

"Not a snowflake's chance in hell, sweetheart," he told me. "I've been happily sequestered here all night, but I'm not hanging out in your lovely house while you face down a bunch of moon-psychotic werewolves solo."

I bristled. "I can handle myself."

I was pretty sure I couldn't, and having a demon along to ride shotgun and have my back, would make me feel better, but I wasn't about to admit that to Lucien.

"I know you can, but why should you have all the fun?" He cracked his knuckles. "If you haven't remembered, I do like to kick some werewolf ass. And as the demon who had a gallon of blood dumped in his hotel room, I'm keen to know who's trying to frame me for this might-be-murder."

He had a point. And I did need back-up. Yes, I had six sisters, but showing up with a whole coven of witches in tow wouldn't get me any cooperation from the werewolves. Of course, showing up with a demon in tow might not either, but I was banking on Dallas not taking Lucien as seriously as he would seven witches on his doorstep.

CHAPTER 14

*D*allas was happy to let me into the compound. He wasn't so happy about Lucien, and I got the impression that his dislike was equally balanced between Lucien being a demon, and Lucien not being a female he could attempt to bang.

Werewolves. The dogs would screw anything female. The bitches were only allowed to have sex with male werewolves. It drove me nuts to have this misogynist crap right here in Accident, but that's the way it had always been. And unless I wanted to pick up my broomstick, put on my pointy hat, and pick this mountain to die on, that's the way it was going to continue.

"The sheriff's already been here," Dallas told me. "Don't know where Clinton is. He didn't come home last night."

"Sure you guys didn't have a challenge fight a day early?" I asked. "Couldn't wait one more day until the full moon?"

Dallas got a rather exasperated look on his face. "If I'd killed Clinton in a challenge fight, I'd have no reason to hide it, let alone haul a bunch of blood into town to try and frame a demon. We're allowed pack law here on the mountain, and challenge duels aren't murder. Besides, Clinton hasn't announced a challenge for this month." The older werewolf shrugged. "I know it's coming, and it's coming soon, but Clinton's got enough sense to do things by the book—and so do I."

"So then where is he?" I insisted. Dallas didn't seem all that concerned that his second and son was missing. Sheriff Oakes had to have told him about all the blood. Wasn't the werewolf the slightest bit worried?

"Full moon is tonight. I've got no idea where half my pack's been the last few days." Dallas turned and howled. Seconds later there were a dozen werewolves standing in the room, eyeing their alpha nervously.

"That's the wolf who was with Clinton outside of the tavern, when we were having our little disagreement," Lucien said, pointing out Shelby.

The werewolf bared her teeth. "I was. Dusted him off and got a smack in my face for the effort. Last I saw Clinton he was walking down the road. Why? Did he come back and kick your ass?"

I stepped between the two, trying to make sure Lucien didn't start another fight with yet another werewolf right in their own compound. "Was he with anyone else? Say where he was going?"

Shelby shook her head then glanced over at Dallas. The alpha confirmed that none of the other wolves had seen Clinton, then dismissed them.

"He'll show up eventually," Dallas said, walking us to the door.

I glanced back at Shelby who was climbing the stairs. "Didn't she challenge Clinton for second a few years back?"

"Yes, and lost," Dallas scoffed. "She's a good fighter. Got real guts. Wouldn't have mattered if she'd won. No one would have followed her anyway."

"Because she's female?" I bristled.

"That and she doesn't know her place. Disrespects the rules. Came close to putting her down a few months back, but I like to give the girls a second chance, you know?"

I knew I wanted to put my fist through this werewolf's face, is what I knew. Or set his pants on fire. Grandma may have worried she wasn't strong enough to take on the werewolves solo, but I wasn't solo, and it was a different time than when Grandma was young.

It was time for a change in Accident. But first I had to find Clinton Dickskin.

Dallas walked us to my car, hovering nearby as Lucien climbed into the passenger side.

"Thought you were gonna get rid of him, Cassie?" Dallas said with a nod toward the demon. "He needs to go. Nobody wants a demon in Accident. You get him out of here and I'll take it up with Clinton when he gets back."

"Not your business, Dallas." I told him as I climbed in the car. "The Perkins family decides who can and can't stay in Accident, and as far as I'm concerned, this demon is welcome to visit or reside within our town."

We drove away and Lucien turned to me. "Is that a fact, now?"

"Yes it is."

"And would you want me to stay in Accident? With you?"

I felt my face grow hot. I'd just met him. Heck, I'd slept with him once. And here I was telling him to pretty much move in.

"Yes. I'd like that."

"Good." He looked out the back window at the compound. "Would Dallas really have killed his son in a challenge duel?" Lucien asked.

"Would your father?" I asked in return.

He thought on that a moment. "Probably. Dad didn't get killed, but he did get tossed out."

"With half the business," I countered.

He grinned. "Yes, with half the business—the half no one else knew how to or wanted to run. But demons get killed in hell. I don't think I'd be spared because of whose loins I sprang from."

"Same here. I don't think Dallas would kill Clinton outright, but if the guy didn't accept a defeat, or kept challenging over and over again, then I think Dallas would do it."

"But why would he hide it?"

"He wouldn't. I don't think Dallas has anything to do with Clinton's disappearance." I sighed. "I'm beginning to think that Dallas is right. Clinton will show up eventually."

"So where are we going now?"

"There's a second mystery here. If I can't solve the first, then maybe we can solve the second."

"Which is…?"

"Which is how your coin got on the other side of that deadfall, right where the break in the wards occurred."

It didn't take us long to reach the spot on Beaverton Road where Bronwyn and I had parked just last night. It all looked benign in the sunshine, a bunch of fallen trees and brambles at the end of a dirt road. Lucien and I got out of the car and walked over, standing in front of the mess.

"So, walk me through the fight again. That's when you lost the coin?"

"I'm assuming so. I had it earlier when we were in the bar drinking, because I was joking that it wouldn't buy me much in the way of beer. I showed it to Alberta and John, and they bought my beer. I had the fight with Clinton right after that. So I'm thinking it fell out of my pocket."

There was an odd expression on his face, as if he didn't

quite believe that. "It fell out of your pocket. Is that even possible?"

"I didn't think it was, but here in this town all sorts of impossible things happen," he joked. "I've got practically no powers here. The coin doesn't even seem to be working. I guess it could have fallen out. Outside of Accident, I would have figured nothing outside of magic would get that coin out of my possession."

"So someone picked it up. Clinton, John, Alberta, Shelby, or any random patron who happened to walk through the parking lot and see a brass coin in the gravel."

He nodded. "Picked it up. Evidently came here. Dropped it."

I eyed the deadfall. "Dropped it on the other side of that mess of downed trees and brambles. This is where the break in the wards was, and where we found your coin."

"And this has nothing to do with Clinton's disappearance, aside from the intersecting timelines?" Lucien asked.

"I'm not sure." Was the break in the wards and the coin related to Clinton's disappearance and possible exsanguination? As it stood, all I had were some rather suspicious coincidences.

"Clearly Clinton wasn't stabbed, or whatever, here or you and Brownwyn would have seen blood," Lucien conjectured. "I lost my coin, or someone picked my pocket, while I was fighting with Clinton. Coincidence? Or not?"

"A lost coin, a missing werewolf, and a broken ward. I've got no idea," I confessed. "Wards don't usually break, and it's just weird that your coin would be here."

"Think someone planted it here?" he asked. "Like the blood in my hotel room? They knew you'd come to investigate a break, and figured they'd pin this on me as well?"

I shrugged. "The blood in the hotel room wasn't done by someone used to manufacturing a crime scene according to

Ophelia. If this was intentional, then it strikes me as a bit amateur as well. I mean, why drop the coin on the other side of the deadfall and the wards, making it look as if you'd escaped, when whoever did this clearly wanted it to appear that you murdered Clinton in your hotel room?"

"Maybe they were going for me killing Clinton in my hotel room, then dragging him all the way across town and throwing him over the deadfall to break the wards, then climbing through, dropping my coin, and dragging Clinton's body off into the woods."

"That's ridiculous." I gestured to the deadfall. "Besides, a bloody werewolf body isn't going to break the wards. Werewolves as well as any of the supernatural residents of the town, are able to come and go through the wards without any hinderance. They suffer a slight degradation in power within the city limits, but that's it. And being dead or covered in blood doesn't change that."

"So what *would* break the wards like this?" Lucien asked.

"Bronwyn and I figured it was a fae. Pixies. Elves. That sort of thing. They can come and go without problem, but their magic can really screw stuff up. The easiest explanation is that a fairy or some type of fae was doing magic, or carrying an enchanted object across the wards, and basically it was like blowing a fuse."

Lucien looked down at his ankle monitor. "An enchanted object like this?"

"With fae, who knows? Maybe. That device was made by Bronwyn, so the magic is compatible with the wards. The wards trigger the anklet and keep you from leaving or passing through them. Fae magic and their enchanted objects are different and not compatible with what we witches do. Sparks fly when our magic gets together, and not in a good way."

"It was dark when you were here last. Maybe something

got overlooked." Lucien jumped up on top of the deadfall. I felt something like a tickle in the back of my brain, then watched as the demon bounced off the invisible wall of the ward to land inelegantly on his feet once more beside me.

"Can you take this damned thing off?" he gestured to his pant leg. "It's not like I'm going anywhere."

There was a magical "key" that was kept at the police station as well as one with the sheriff. Bronwyn could deactivate it with a word since she was the one that enchanted the device.

And so could I. I'd grown up with Bronwyn, shared a bedroom with her. I knew her magic as well as I knew my own. Of all my sisters, hers was the magic I felt the most in tune with.

I eyed the silver peeking out from under his pants' hem. In the last twenty-four hours I'd had more doings with magic than I had in the last year. I could lie and just let him wear the darned thing until the law removed it. I could insist he just sprout those wings of his and fly over the wards. I'm pretty sure if he wanted to, he could smash right through the wards. He was a demon. I didn't know much about their magic, but from what I'd read, I bet it made fae magic look like a kid's birthday party entertainment. But him smashing through the wards would mean my sisters and I would need to repair them. And I'd really hate to explain to Bronwyn that the reason we were doing all this work on a Saturday morning was because I was too damned lazy to take her enchanted anklet off this demon.

"Hold still." I knelt down, trying not to get my knees in the dirt as I felt around the silver band for the invisible clasp. With a word the device clicked free, two pieces of metal in my hands. Lucien reached down to rub his leg while I tossed the device in the car. By the time I'd returned, the demon was on top of the deadfall. There was a tiny scrap of fabric in his hand.

"Think if you got this to your sister Ophelia, she could tell us who it belongs to?" he asked.

I took it from him and squinted. How the hell had he found this in a huge pile of branches and mud? It looked to be from a pair of blue jeans. I'd been wearing a pantsuit last night, and hadn't climbed the deadfall. Bronwyn had been wearing tan Carhartt pants. But who was to say this hadn't been left here weeks or months ago, and had nothing to do with Clinton Dickskin's disappearance?

"I'll check with Ophelia," I told the demon. I'd check with her later, just in case this didn't go anywhere. She was probably finally getting some sleep after her night on-call at the firehouse and I wouldn't want to wake her for what might end up being a dead end.

"Any blood or anything?" I called up. "How sensitive is a demon's nose? Werewolf-quality? Because I'm hoping you can grab a scent and follow a trail."

He continued to slowly make his way across the deadfall. "Not in my skillset. Can we call in a werewolf though? They've got an interest in finding out where Clinton is. Maybe they can check for his scent here and track him, or his body, down."

"You heard Dallas. They think he's sleeping it off somewhere and don't care enough to go find him. Maybe if he doesn't show up in a week or two, they'll go looking." Actually, they might not even in that case. Clinton had a handful of supporters, sycophants who felt he was going to be their next alpha and wanted to lay the groundwork for their own self-advancement. Other than that, a good bit of the pack hated him. Of course, a good bit of the pack hated Dallas as well. That seemed to be the case with werewolf packs. There wasn't a lot of love going on there, even among mated pairs.

"Find anything else?" I asked.

He scrambled down the deadfall and held something out to me. "Only this."

It was a seed bead. Gold with a swirl of green. And the magic of it crawled up my fingers clear to my wrist. Fae magic.

And suddenly I realized I'd been ignoring what was right in front of me the whole time.

"We need to go visit Alberta," I told Lucien.

"Why?" He looked down at the bead as I held it up.

"Because she's a troll. And trolls are fae. And I'm pretty sure this bead is from her bracelet."

CHAPTER 15

When Cassie had said the troll lived under a bridge, I'd thought…I don't know, maybe something like one of those homeless tent-cities between the concrete supports of a highway overpass? I hadn't expected an adorable stone bungalow tucked in beside a creek. There was indeed a bridge that went over the back part of the roof and over the creek before winding through the woods on the other side, but it looked as if it rarely saw any traffic.

"My favorite color is blue," Cassie shouted as she knocked on the door. I must have given her a perplexed look because she turned to me with a grin and told me it was from a movie.

Alberta opened the door, clearly nervous.

Cassie held out the bead. "You broke the wards, Alberta."

The troll squirmed. "There's lots of people that have beads like that," she countered.

"I did a spell. It's yours."

I shot Cassie an appreciative glance. She'd lied.

Alberta clearly didn't know that. She looked down at her feet. "It's not against the rules for me to leave the town. I can come and go as I please. Not my fault the wards broke. They do that sometimes with fae."

"With fae who are in the middle of casting a spell, or carrying a fae-enchanted object that's been activated," Cassie countered. "What were you doing Alberta?"

"None of your business." The troll tried to close the door and I stuck my foot in to block it.

"Does it have something to do with this?" I showed her my coin.

Her eyes widened. "I didn't steal it. I promise I didn't steal it. I found it and it's mine. I was taking it to my special place. That's why I crossed the wards. I didn't steal. And I get to come and go whenever I please. I did nothing wrong."

Cagey. Defensive. One didn't have to be a demon to know that this troll had been up to something she really didn't want Cassie knowing about. And I got the feeling it wasn't about my coin either.

"I don't want people to find my treasures, you know?" Alberta continued. "Especially the fairies. They think I keep everything here under my bridge, and I know sometimes they search for stuff, so I have a secret hiding place."

Cassie got an unreadable, carefully blank expression on her face that I was certain worked in the courtroom. It definitely worked on me. "Why have your treasure place outside the town limits? On the other side of the wards?"

Alberta squirmed. "No one looks there. And my magic is full-force outside the wards, so I can safeguard my special place and the wards don't interfere with that."

I assumed that meant it would be hard for anyone to find outside of a witch casting a divination spell. Even another fae would most likely struggle to see through a troll's glamour.

"Where is Clinton Dickskin?" I asked the troll, taking the sort of tone I used when interrogating, punishing actually, souls in hell.

Both women flinched. Alberta whimpered, then seemed to get control of herself.

"Clinton is missing? When did he go missing?"

Fae. They couldn't lie, but they could dance around the truth like nobody's business. One of the reasons I avoided them like the plague.

"Did you put Clinton's blood into Lucien's hotel room?" Cassie took over. Again I imagined her questioning witnesses in the courtroom, setting her ex's pants on fire. This needed to wrap up and soon so I could get her back home and into bed.

"No, I didn't put Clinton's blood into Lucien's hotel room," Alberta squeaked.

"Were you there when someone else put Clinton's blood into Lucien's hotel room?"

"No."

"Do you know who put Clinton's blood into Lucien's hotel room?"

"No. I wasn't there. I don't know who did that. Check with Dallas, or someone in his pack. I was there last night outside the tavern when Lucien and Clinton fought. When they all scattered, I picked up the coin Lucien dropped." She shot the demon a nervous glance. "It wasn't stealing. When you lose something, it's fair game."

I didn't care. The damned thing didn't seem to be working, and it wasn't like I was in a hurry to return to hell any time in the near future. I was more curious how it had gotten out of my pocket without my removing it.

"So you went back inside to have a drink with Lucien and John, then left them to head to your hidey-hole?" Cassie asked, her eyes narrowing.

The troll squirmed. "No. I had it in my pocket for a while."

"Where did you go directly after the fight at the tavern?"

She glared. "I'm not telling you. That's private. It's none of your business."

"I can make you tell me, Alberta, but I'd prefer not to. Where did you go directly after the fight at the tavern?"

I glanced at Cassie in surprise. Had she just threatened to go all law-and-order on the troll? Was she finally taking her place as head witch of this town? If that was the case, then I was definitely staying. Cassie in bed with me was incredible. Cassie as a witch, partnering with me, sharing energy in spells, was just as incredible. Seeing her like this—confident, skilled, taking charge… It made me realize I wanted more than a partnership with this witch, I wanted an eternity.

Alberta didn't find Cassie's threat as erotically compelling as I did. The troll puffed up her chest and glared back at the witch. "That's illegal. You can't do that to me. The sheriff would need to arrest me, and I'd get a lawyer—a lawyer that isn't you. And there's no cause to arrest me."

"Technically you're right. Our law enforcement *is* modeled on a human system, and since Grandma's death, there hasn't been any deviation from that system." Cassie took a step forward, her foot crossing the threshold. "Until now. You can tell me or I can make you tell me. Those are your options, and afterward if you want to go complain to the sheriff, you can. But remember that living in Accident is a privilege, Alberta. It's a privilege that can easily be revoked if I find there's been a murder and you've not cooperated with the investigation."

The expression on the troll's face said everything. Cassie had done it. She'd just taken her place as the witch that ran things in this town. There was no backing down for her now.

Or for me.

"I'm not involved in a murder." The troll's voice was a panicked whisper. "Don't kick me out, Cassie. Don't. I'm not involved in any murder. I picked up the coin, then I joined my lover for a while. I don't want to name who that is because there are complications—complications that can get them seriously hurt or even killed. Please don't force me to tell you who I was with. And please don't kick me out of the town."

Cassie's expression momentarily softened. "I don't want to kick you out Alberta. And I don't want to get your lover strung up for cheating on his or her wife with you. There was a lot of blood in that hotel room. We're worried about Clinton. He might be a total ass, but he's still a resident of this town and we need to make sure he's okay."

The troll began to cry. Huge watery tears soaked her face and the front of her shirt. It was like watching a river pour down someone's face. Cassie dug in her pockets for a Kleenex, handing it over to Alberta. It didn't help much. With a few gulps, the troll got control of herself, wiping her face with the sodden, shredded tissue.

"I hate Clinton. I hate him. But I'm not a murderer. I'm not," she insisted with a warble in her voice. "I'm telling you right now that I didn't kill him. I can't lie. I'm a fae and I can't lie. I didn't kill Clinton."

"Okay, okay. I believe you," Cassie patted her on the shoulder. "So after you left your lover? Then what? Tell me what happened?"

Alberta swallowed hard. "After we parted, I went to take my treasure to my special place. And crossing the deadfall, I snagged my bracelet and dropped the coin. I went to my special place and realized that I'd lost the coin. Then I came straight back to my bridge here, and didn't leave for the rest of the night."

I was sure she was telling the truth, but something about the way she'd worded it bothered me. Was this really what had happened. Did Alberta have nothing to do with Clinton? Had she just picked up the fallen coin, gone to rock the sheets with whoever she was banging, then gone to stash the coin in her secret place?

Cassie eyed the troll. "So you didn't see Clinton Dickskin again after the fight outside the tavern was over?"

"Last time I saw Clinton Dickskin, he was alive. He was bloody and had the crap beaten out of him, but he was alive. If he's dead, then I had nothing to do with it," Alberta proclaimed.

Which wasn't exactly what Cassie had asked. She thanked the troll for her cooperation and we headed back to her car.

"She knows what happened to Clinton." I mused. "He was alive when she last saw him, but maybe someone killed him after that—someone who was also responsible for dumping a bucket of the werewolf's blood on the floor of my hotel room."

Cassie nodded. "I agree. I could pry the information out of her, but I really don't want to burn that bridge right now, and I'm not sure what sort of magical toll it would take on me to ferret answers out of a reluctant fae."

"With my help? Not much of a toll at all." I halted her, taking her arms in my hands. "Cassie, your magic calls to me. It begs me to share myself with you. This is the bond between a witch and a demon. This is why covens over the centuries have summoned demons. This is why a bonding, a partnership with a demon is so valuable—for both of us."

She reached out to put her hands on my waist. "It's not just the magical toll, Lucien. I don't want to do that to Alberta. I don't want to start off throwing my witch-weight around like that. I don't want people in this town to be afraid of me, like I'm some powerful dictator with a demon to back me up. Yes, I'll use force if absolutely necessary. But that needs to be a last result, not my first action. Does that make sense?"

No, but if that's the way she wanted to run her town, then

I wasn't going to argue. Things were different in hell, but I wasn't in hell. And I was more interested in supporting Cassie and being her partner in all ways then arguing with her about the proper use of forceful magic.

I kissed her lightly, giving her bottom lip a quick nip with my teeth as I pulled away. "Okay, sweetheart. Just know that I'm here and ready to go whenever you need me. Like a demon battery."

"Hopefully one of those go-all-night batteries." She smacked my ass and headed to the driver's side of the car. "But that's later—*after* we find Clinton Dickskin."

I was suddenly very motivated to find Clinton Dickskin.

"So Alberta saw Clinton after the fight, and he was alive," I commented as we drove away from the troll's bridge. "Am I reading that right? Troll speak?"

"You're reading that right." Cassie turned the car away from town and back toward the forest. "She's got a forbidden lover she can't, or won't, name—one that she saw after the fight and before she went to hide my coin with her other treasures. By her timeline, she would have had to have seen Clinton while she was with her 'lover', while she was over at the deadfall, or afterward when she was home the rest of the night."

"Let's consider the first one," I said. "Clinton is her secret lover. She gets carried away and seriously injures him. Hides him in a panic while he's still clinging to life, then frames me for it with a bucket of blood."

"She didn't have anything to do with or knowledge about the bucket of blood," Cassie corrected me. "Fae can't lie, and even if she could, I believe Alberta on that one. Besides, as rough as trolls can get in the sack, and I do *not* know that from personal experience, werewolves are hardy. She wouldn't have almost killed Clinton hanging him, especially the night before the full moon when the wolves are at their strongest."

I shrugged. "She just said she was with her lover, not what they were doing. What if she was out at another bar with this lover, and Clinton happened to be there all beat up?"

"Then she would have used the bar as an alibi and not risk exposing her 'lover,'" Cassie countered. "If she took the risk to mention the lover, then she was probably alone with him or her and that's her only alibi."

"Okay. Scenario two, she saw Clinton at the deadfall." I ticked the number off on my fingers. "She was dropping off her treasure, and there he was."

"Doing what? What would Clinton be doing out there?" Cassie snorted. "It was the night before the full moon. He'd be either fighting, hunting, or screwing."

"Hunting?" I suggested. "Tracking a deer and he runs across Alberta?"

"Maybe she was on her way, ran into Clinton, then got freaked out that he'd know where she stashed her treasures?"

"And killed him rather than have him reveal her secrets?" I nodded. "She claims she didn't have anything to do with the blood at my hotel room, but maybe she killed Clinton, freaked out and told her lover, and this lover covered it all up for her?"

Cassie laughed. "First off, although I'm positive that trolls can kill, and that under the right circumstances, Alberta could kill, I don't think she'd whack Clinton over that. Especially because Clinton wouldn't give a crap about her treasure stuff. Alberta doesn't even register on his radar. Besides if he saw her hidey hole, she'd just move her stuff elsewhere, not attack him. And as I said before, Clinton is a werewolf one night away from the monthly event that makes shifters pretty close to unbeatable. Alberta is young for a troll.

There's a slim chance she could have prevailed, but she would have been sporting a whole lot of cuts and bruises."

I nodded. "Maybe she had help. Her and her lover were out at the deadfall or wherever her secret stash is. They run across Clinton. Kill him, or almost kill him. Leave him in the woods and the lover covers it up."

Cassie bit her lip, a frown creasing her forehead. With a deft twist of the wheel, she turned the car down a side road. "I still don't think Alberta would kill or even whack Clinton over his knowing where her hidey-hole is."

"But his knowing who her lover is…?" I shot Cassie a knowing glance.

"I can't see Clinton giving two shits about a married guy cheating on his spouse with Alberta, but maybe in a panic…" She shook her head. "None of these sounds right to me, but I'm concerned enough that Clinton may be lying in the woods bleeding out a few hundred yards from that deadfall that I'm going to head back and check things out more thoroughly. Got any more theories, hellboy?"

"I have *all* the theories," I told her. "Scenario three, or is it four, is where Alberta sees Clinton going out to her treasure spot, they hook up, and he spends the night with her. He's right now at her hidey hole in a sex coma, waiting for Alberta to come back with bacon and eggs for round two."

Cassie burst out laughing. "Okay, that's one that I actually like."

I waved a finger, making an additional point. "Alberta wouldn't mention where Clinton is because her other forbidden lover might get jealous. I'll bet he turns up in a few hours minus his pants, a shit-eating grin on his face."

She chuckled. "Except none of that explains Clinton's blood in your bedroom. He doesn't roll like that sexually, and Alberta denied having anything to do with that. Besides,

Clinton isn't exactly Alberta's type. Although I'm the first to admit shifters have a certain sort of appeal."

I let out a growl at that statement.

"Not as much appeal as demons," she added with a grin.

Good. "So you think Clinton may be out in the woods somewhere?"

"Possibly." She glanced over at me. "That offer you made? The one about helping me with a spell? Think I'd like to take you up on that."

"A spell to get the truth out of Alberta?" I asked.

"No, a spell to see where she's been."

I nodded. "Your wish is my command, sweetheart."

"She only said she saw him alive. That could have been *after* someone drained a gallon of blood out of him," Cassie said. "It fits the timeline better if she stumbled across him while returning from her treasure spot."

"So Alberta came across a terribly injured Clinton in the woods and just walked away?" I shook my head. "Wow, and they call *us* demons."

"You're right. I can't see her doing that." Cassie frowned in thought. "I can't see her just leaving him lying there, but in all honestly, trolls don't think of physical injury the same way that humans, or even werewolves do. Her idea of medical care would have been…interesting."

I reached out to rest my hand on her thigh. "I've gotta say, this has got to be the most fun I've had since the French revolution. Bring it on Cassie. What's our next step here? How are you going to do this spell?"

"Some rocks. You. And…" She winked and held up her hand. "This."

"A hair?"

"A troll hair to be exact. *Alberta's* troll hair."

"You stole a hair. You stood there in her doorway and… what, plucked it out of her head? Off her sweater? What?"

"I'm not revealing my hair-stealing secrets to you," she teased. "Anyway, we're going to go back to the deadfall. I'm going to cast a spell with your help. And we're going to trace that troll's steps. Maybe we'll find a cave full of treasure. Maybe we'll find an injured werewolf. Maybe we'll find nothing."

I nodded. "I've got a feeling in my leathery wings we're going to find something."

"So do I, hellboy." She nodded. "So do I."

CHAPTER 16

CASSANDRA

The moment I'd announced I was going to do a spell, I'd felt this electric charge. Something about crossing this line energized me. And it seemed to have done the same to Lucien. It was as if I'd been talking dirty, or promising him sexual favors. He'd sucked in a breath, and barely been able to keep his eyes from me as I drove to the deadfall. As soon as we got out of my car, he'd come around the side and walked close to me, heat radiating off his body. I swear I could feel his wings, feel the intensity of his demonic energy. It stirred my blood, made me want to screw him in the back seat of my car. But I had a spell to do and a werewolf, alive or dead, to find, and something about that was just as sexually charged as the idea of fucking Lucien in my car.

I'd come woefully unprepared for this. Bronwyn and Ophelia carried spell components with them all the time. I obviously didn't. But unlike my sisters, I could work my shit on the fly. It would be difficult. It would take more energy. But it could be done. And with this demon next to me, charging me up and making me feel breathless and aware, I felt as if I could rule the world.

"I'm so going to fuck you after this," he breathed as I gathered some stones and sticks and arranged them in the appropriate fashion.

"Are you like this with all the witches, or just me?" I teased. Sorta teased. I'll admit this sort of fascination and attention was heady, but I'd been burned before. It would suck if he just got it on with any witch he came across, much like Marcus had got it on with any female, or male, he'd come across.

He hesitated. "There's an undeniable attraction between demons and witches. It's been going on since time began. Every demon's dream is to be summoned into a coven, to gather those witches to his side and experience the joy that happens every time they cast a spell, every time they offer their bodies to him or her. There's something electric about a witch that every demon longs to experience."

My heart fell a few feet. "And there's seven of us in this town. We're like a buffet here."

He grabbed my arm and pulled me over, gathering me into his arms. "You're more than some damned buffet, Cassie. I knew the moment I met you that there was something special between us—something once-in-a-lifetime between us. You're more than just a witch. You're more than a coven of witches. You're someone to walk by my side, to share the joy of hell with."

Hell? Wasn't sure I wanted to think about what he might mean about that one. "So you'd consider an exclusive physical and emotional relationship?" Because after Marcus, there's no way I could deal with sharing anyone I cared about. Next time there would be more than pants set on fire here.

Lucien grinned then kissed me. When he finally let me up

for air, he placed his forehead against mine. "Do your magic witch. Let me soak it all in. Let me savor every moment of it all. And tonight, when we're alone, I'll return the favor."

I pulled away, flustered. I'd had some really damned good sex with Marcus, but nothing like this—nothing like the sense of connection, or worshipful admiration that I got from this demon.

Trying to clear my head, I finished placing the stones and sticks, then placed Alberta's hair in the center of it all and began to chant. The ground surged beneath me. The air thickened and throbbed. I heard Lucien catch his breath and suddenly the energy I held deep inside my core surged forth in a wave.

The path became clear in my mind—as clear as if I'd seen it on a Google map highlighted in red.

"She crossed the deadfall," I told Lucien, my voice foggy as if in a trance. I scrambled across the branches and dead-wood, barely aware of the hand steadying my way. Then I wandered through the trees and marshy land, my shoes becoming thick with coated mud as I walked. In the back of my mind I wondered at Alberta, a troll, crossing such a wet terrain. Trolls were earth-bound—one of the few fae who were. Alberta lost every bit of her power over water, and would have suffered a reduction of her abilities in such wet land. Dry ground and stone were a troll's strength. This wet land…it didn't make sense. Unless Alberta was really serious about hiding whatever treasures she had from other earth-bound supernatural creatures like ogres and goblins.

About fifty yards through the damp forest I realized something. The trail I was following was thick. Fat. Wide. Alberta wasn't a svelte woman, but even in her natural troll form, this seemed to be more of a magical swath than she should have been creating. The realization made me catch my breath. And hurry.

Lucien followed me, silent, intent, his arousal like a caress on my skin. I tried to ignore him and concentrated on the magical pathway weaving its way along the trees and brush. Finally we came to a cliff face, a sheer rock wall that rose a good thirty feet straight up before angling off into a stony terrain of pine. I looked upward, wondering how Alberta could have managed something that should have required ropes and skilled climbing technique.

"Fae," Lucien whispered. "Think like a fae."

Glamour. Fae were all about glamour. Outside of Accident, trolls relied on it the most, making their appearance more acceptable to humans and hiding their dwellings from the rest of the world. Alberta would use the same in concealing her special hiding place. Concentrating, I closed my eyes and centered. And when I opened them, I saw the entrance.

With a word I'd dispelled the illusion, and before us was a two-foot opening through the rock.

I swayed and Lucien took my arm. "You okay?"

I nodded, feeling far from okay. I'd spent the last fifteen years of my life actively not practicing magic. I had power. I had skill. And I was woefully out of practice. There was a deep well of energy within me, but tapping it made me feel weak and shaky. Out here alone, I would have probably headed back, but with Lucien by my side, I felt as if I could continue. He would help me. He would protect me. He'd make sure I made it out of here even if I passed out.

Lucien helped me scramble up the rocky path to the opening, then he hovered nearby as I knelt down to crawl through the opening. Inside was pitch black, so I hesitated and dug my cell phone out of my pocket, clicking on the flashlight app. Ahead of me was a two-foot pathway ending in what looked to be a cavern. I crawled forward, shining my light upward. The cavern was about four feet high, and six by eight feet wide. Along the walls were strings of beads, pictures and paintings, statues and pottery. All the sorts of things I'd expected a troll might consider her treasures. And laying on the ground beneath it all was a very pale werewolf.

"Lucien!" I shouted. "Help me!"

The demon was right behind me, but the passage was narrow and he had to practically knock me over to get past me into the cavern. Once there, he sucked in his breath upon seeing the werewolf illuminated by the faint light of my flashlight app.

He knelt down beside Clinton and ripped the duct tape off the werewolf's mouth. Clinton moaned, his head lolling to the side.

"Hold the flashlight steady," Lucien commanded as he tore through the excessive amount of tape and rope used to bind the werewolf. Well, excessive for a human. I guess for a werewolf, it was probably a prudent amount.

The beam of my flashlight revealed that Clinton hadn't just lost a ton of blood and been bound, he'd had the crap beat out of him. And I was thinking all these wounds weren't from his run in with Lucien outside of the tavern last night.

"Can you get him out of here? He'll heal quicker outside."

Lucien knelt down and pulled the werewolf across his shoulders, army crawling his way through the entrance to keep from smashing the comatose werewolf against the stone roof. Once outside, he laid him down on the mossy ground while I came out of the cavern.

"Damn Alberta," I raged staring down at the pale, bloodied, unconscious werewolf. "She lied."

"Technically, she didn't." Lucien's voice was droll.

I scampered over to Clinton, checked his vitals, relieved to feel a steady pulse. "We need to get him out of here." I glanced down the wet muddy trail to where the deadfall was. Even if I could get my car over the deadfall, I'd never make it through this mud. But clearly Clinton wasn't walking on his own two feet out of here.

"I got this." Huge wings snapped out from Lucien's back. "I can't carry you both, so I'll fly him out to your car."

"I'll meet you there," I told him, jumping up and getting a head start. As much as I wanted the experience of being flown around in a demon's arms, I didn't want Clinton being unattended until I was sure he was okay—and until I was sure no one would come by and finish him off.

I was out of breath and covered in mud by the time I made it back over the deadfall to see Lucien standing next to Clinton. He'd laid the werewolf onto the ground next to my car, and I winced thinking that the demon looked rather menacing looming over the werewolf like that.

I checked Clinton's vitals again and sent Ophelia a text. Normally I'd call Dallas for the werewolves to take care of their own, but until I knew exactly who had done this, I didn't trust anyone beyond my own sisters. And Lucien.

"You think Alberta did this?" Lucien asked.

I shook my head. "No, I don't think so. I don't see her as a killer."

I did see her as someone who would stash a seriously injured werewolf somewhere out of the way, not thinking that he might possibly die out there. But why? There had to be a good reason for Alberta to want to hide an injured Clinton away where he couldn't be found.

Because she'd known who did this and had a vested interest in protecting them, but wasn't so morally depraved that she really wanted Clinton to die.

I knelt down beside Clinton, peeling away his tattered clothes and assessing his injuries. There were bruises and cuts whose level of healing lead me to believe they'd occurred around twenty-four hours ago. There were some broken bones that had begun to knit—probably a half hour to two hours before his last devastating injury depending on how bad those injuries had been. Then there was a puncture wound that probably should have killed him.

The werewolf's eyes popped open and I caught my breath.

"Bitch," he breathed, pink liquid bubbling from his lips.

"Alberta?" I asked. "Who did this, Clinton? Who did this to you?"

His eyes wandered to Lucien, then widened when he saw the demon's wings. "I repent. I repent. Don't take me. Don't. Done some bad things, but not that bad. Want to repent."

Lucien rolled his eyes. "Oh, the deathbed confession. Screw you, dude. Much to my regret, you're going to make it this time."

"I repent," Clinton insisted.

"Not my call," Lucien informed him. "I just deal out the punishment, I don't decide who deserves it."

Clinton gasped and I shot Lucien a warning glance. "Who did this?" I asked the werewolf. "Clinton. Stay with me. Who did this?"

"Got jumped."

"After the fight with Lucien at the tavern?" I asked. "Where did you go? Do you know who attacked you?"

He frowned. "Walked down the road a bit. Something with claws. And magic."

I exchanged a puzzled glance with Lucien. "Claws and magic?"

"Claws stabbed. Something hit me. One attacker I think. Then nothing. Magic and nothing." He winced and coughed, spitting some blood onto the ground. "I think a magic spell knocked me out, 'cause I don't remember fighting, just getting attacked, then nothing until just now."

He closed his eyes and his head lolled to the side. I wasn't alarmed since already the werewolf was breathing easier, a bit of color beginning to return to this skin. The power of the full moon. Even in the daylight, this time of the month, a werewolf would heal just about any injury. Must be nice.

"Magic," Lucien mused. "The attacker used magic to subdue him."

"Which means whoever attacked him didn't have enough strength to take Clinton down solo without a spell." I held up my hands. "That could be just about anyone in town. Clinton has pissed off most of the residents of Accident at one time or another."

"But which of those have access to magic?" Lucien prodded.

I frowned in thought. "Bronwyn is pretty selective about who gets her enchanted devices. I really doubt this is her, and none of my sisters outside of Bronwyn and I could enchant something with a long-lasting sleep spell like this. So that leaves…"

"Fae." Lucien completed my thought.

"Fae," I agreed. "It seems Alberta assisted in this assault as well as taking Clinton and stashing him with her treasure. But was Clinton supposed to die and no one find the body? Or maybe he was just supposed to be hidden away until after the full moon?"

"To keep him from fighting with Dallas for pack alpha?" Lucien asked. "There's someone who doesn't want Clinton as pack alpha?"

"That would only delay things for a month." I shook my head. "No, I really think Clinton was supposed to die last night."

The demon looked down at the werewolf. "We should consider that Alberta's the reason he's still alive. I get the impression she stashed him to keep whoever from finishing him off."

"She thought the assault was only to teach Clinton a lesson, but got alarmed when the assailant took it too far," I mused, thinking this was very much in keeping with the Alberta I knew. "Instead of disposing of a body where no one could find it, she ties and duct-tapes Clinton and hauls him out with her treasure."

"But to do what?" Lucien laughed. "Was she planning on keeping him there forever? She must have known that eventually she'd either have to kill him or let him go."

I smiled. "That's Alberta. She doesn't always think ahead. I'm sure she was hoping she could smooth things over with the assailant then set Clinton free."

"And why would she think that?"

"Because the assailant is her lover," I told Lucien. "Alberta would do a lot for her friends, but she'll do anything for a romantic partner—anything except murder evidently."

"And she's made it quite clear she's not going to tell you who that lover is."

I smiled. "She doesn't have to. I already know who her lover is. And I intend on confronting the pair of them."

"And punishing them?" Lucien purred, clearly excited about that idea.

"No." I hated to disappoint the demon, but this town had seen enough violence. And if things had gone down the way I was thinking, then Alberta and her lover had good reason for wanting Clinton dead.

It was something pretty darned close to self-defense. And self-defense against a werewolf, or even a pack alpha, sometimes involved murder.

CHAPTER 17

CASSANDRA

Ophelia showed up with an ambulance and her crew from the firehouse to haul Clinton off to what passed for a hospital in Accident. We didn't often have need for things like surgery or long-term medical care, but even supernaturals had the occasional emergency. With the full moon tonight, Clinton would most likely be up and out harassing everyone by tomorrow morning. In fact, now that he was out of Alberta's cave and free from whatever sedation spell she'd most likely cast on him, he was clearly doing better.

Heck, he might even be out at the bars tonight. One thing he didn't have, though, was a memory of who or what attacked him. In fact, his memory of the events prior to his attack were still fuzzy. I wasn't sure if he'd get those back or not.

I hoped not.

We drove up to the werewolf compound. For once, Dallas didn't answer the door. This time it was just the werewolf I wanted to see—Shelby.

"Why don't the three of us take a walk?" I told her. "Away from other ears."

She glanced back, then nodded. We passed my car and were about two hundred yards from the main house when she turned to face me.

"Yes, I killed him. Alberta knows nothing about any of this. It has nothing to do with her. It was a fight, and I killed Clinton. And I'll face pack law for it."

Her chin came up with the last statement. Pack law would have meant no punishment if it had been a fair challenge.

But it hadn't been a fair challenge.

"I'm not going to argue about whether you should face pack or human law for this right now," I told her. "I just want you to know that we found Clinton. He's not dead, he's injured. And Sheriff Oakes will be arresting Alberta for assault if not attempted murder. We found Clinton in the place where she hides her treasures, sedated, injured, bound, and duct taped."

Shelby paled. "No! She had nothing to do with it. It was me. I…I put Clinton there. She didn't know anything about this."

"But she did," I said as gently as I could. "Alberta was there when you attacked Clinton. She cast that sleep spell on him. Then she hid him away."

"Pack law." Shelby's chin came up. "Any repercussions I face over my…my challenge to Clinton falls under pack law."

"It wasn't a challenge. And Alberta doesn't fall under pack law." I put my hand on her shoulder. "And if what I think is true, then you might not want to find justice under pack law either."

She began to cry. It was a much more subdued sorrow than what Alberta had shown, but there were quite a few tears. And I didn't have any more tissues.

"Either way I'm in trouble," she sniffed. "I might be dead."

"No one is going to be dead," I declared. "Now stop dancing around the truth here and tell me what happened so maybe I can actually help you. And help Alberta."

She gave me a watery smile. "I wasn't supposed to fall in love with a troll, you know. It was a couple of months ago. I'd lost out to Clinton in my bid for pack second, and Dallas had given me this horrible speech about how bitches needed to know their place and maybe if I had a pup or two I'd settle down and not be trying to run things in the pack. That shit-head of a minotaur had just left Alberta. We were both at Pistol Pete's, drinking and complaining. One thing led to another."

"And female werewolves aren't allowed to mate outside of their species," I added softly.

She nodded. "If it had just been the one time, no one would have cared. I mean, I might have gotten my ass beat or confined to the compound for a moon or two, but that would have been it. But it wasn't just once. And Alberta and I... I love her. I know you're probably wondering how someone could love a troll, but she's smart and kind, and wow is she amazing in the sack."

I so didn't need the visual that was running through my head right now. Everyone deserved love. And if it was between a werewolf and a troll...well, more power to them.

"Someone found out and told?" I asked, remembering what Dallas had said about Shelby. He hadn't just been annoyed at her challenging Clinton, he'd been pissed at her more than that.

Shelby sighed. "Yes, someone told. I lied and said it was only the one time. Took my punishment. Swore not to do it again. And I tried. Dallas is mating me off to another wolf next moon. I knew if I got caught again, I'd never be allowed to leave the compound ever. Maybe I'd even be killed. But I couldn't help myself. I love her. And she loves me."

"So ditch the compound and your asshole of an alpha and move in with your troll," Lucien suggested.

"Werewolves don't quit the pack," she told Lucien. "There are no lone wolves here. None. Dallas would never allow it."

"Well, Dallas doesn't run things in this town," I told her. "Tell me what happened last night, and we'll think about what we can do to fix this."

She shook her head. "I'm not sure there's anything anyone can do for me, but here's the truth. Your demon hottie here got into it *again* with Clinton outside the tavern. I dusted him off. He left and I waited for Alberta to come back out. Clinton must have come back for round two because he caught the two of us making out. He grabbed me, was going to haul me back here to Dallas for punishment…"

"So you whacked him," Lucien finished for the wolf.

"Actually, it was Alberta that whacked him. Then I clawed him. And bit him. And Alberta was worried he was getting the upper hand, so she knocked him out with her magic. He was bleeding all over the place, and I didn't have any idea what she'd done. I thought she'd killed him, so I told her to hide the body somewhere that no one would ever find it, took as much of Clinton's blood as I could manage to get out of him, and dumped it in the demon's hotel room." She looked over at Lucien. "Sorry about that."

He shrugged. "Apology accepted."

"Clinton is alive, and he's going to be okay," I told her. "So right now you're looking at assault and Alberta is looking at kidnapping and accessory, even before we get to what you did to Hollister's hotel room."

"Doesn't matter," she countered with a wave of her hand. "Because I'm thinking I'll probably be dead as soon as Clinton tells Dallas I'm sleeping with Alberta."

"Here's your choice." I held up a finger. "Go through our witch-modified human justice system in Accident. Take whatever punishment you get. Break free from the pack and live happily ever after with Alberta. Or avoid any punishment for what happened to Clinton and submit to your alpha and pack law."

She shook her head. "You don't understand. I can't be a lone wolf here. Dallas will come get me. He'll drag me back to the compound. The Perkins witches have never interfered with pack law. They've never enforced their rules over the alphas."

"Well, this Perkins witch is going to do just that," I told her. "I'm sick of those dogs on the mountain getting away with shit, with harassing townspeople and not being held accountable for it. I'm sick of you female werewolves being denied basic rights because of some outdated pack law."

She stared at me, her eyes huge. "Dallas will kill you."

"Over my dead body," Lucien drawled. "I'll see that werewolf in hell before he harms one hair on Cassie's head."

For the first time I saw Shelby actually smile. "Really, Cassie? You'd really do this for me?"

I reached over and grabbed Lucien's hand. "We'll do this for you. Now come on. You and Alberta have got some explaining to do to the sheriff, and after that Lucien and I have to pay a formal visit to your alpha."

We headed to my car, Shelby practically skipping.

"Are they going to handcuff me down at the police station?" she asked.

"Only if you're lucky," I told her.

"Not lucky," Lucien countered, rubbing his wrists. "The handcuffs are enchanted. Not the sexy-time sort of handcuffs at all."

"I don't care," Shelby said as she slid into the back seat of my car. "If I can finally be with Alberta, then they can put all the enchanted handcuffs on me they like."

CHAPTER 18

*S*helby didn't spend long in handcuffs. Clinton regained his senses quicker than expected, although he didn't remember seeing Shelby making out with Alberta. When we told him a sanitized, somewhat non-truthful, version of Shelby getting the upper hand in a challenge fight and Alberta "saving" him and hauling him off before he got killed, he declined to press any charges.

As long as Shelby didn't take his spot as number two in the pack, that is. Clinton really wanted all of this to go away, and not a word of it to be spoken. Anywhere. To anyone. Being beaten by a female werewolf then rescued by a female troll? That was not the sort of thing a bully wanted widely known.

Of course, I was determined to make sure that rumor quickly spread throughout town.

Alberta was off the hook. Shelby was off the hook aside for some hard work at Hollister's to pay him back for trashing room six and ruining his carpet. Everything came up roses.

Well, everything except for our meeting with Dallas, that

is. Let's just say that although Alberta and Shelby were safe from any reprisals, I was pretty sure I wasn't. Good thing I had Lucien by my side, as I'm pretty sure the demon was the main reason I wasn't fighting for my life against the were- wolf alpha right now. I was safe…for now. But I knew I'd need to be watching my step.

As for the rest…well, all my sisters were in the dining room along with Aaron, waiting for Sunday dinner—a dinner I was fixing with the help of Lucien who in three days had become a part of our family.

"So…how long does this vacation of yours last?" I shot him a side-eye while stirring the green beans. "When do you need to be back in hell, torturing lost souls and balancing budgets, or whatever it is the son of Satan does?"

What I really wanted to know was if this was a one-week fling, or something more. I mean, I knew it was "more", just how *much* more? Could I do a long-distance relationship with someone who called hell their home? How often could he be here? Because the idea of staying the night as his place didn't exactly hold much appeal.

Lucien shrugged. "Most demons take a few years off here and there. I could probably be gone a decade, maybe a century if I made it a practice to check in on things every now and then."

"A century?" I let out a breath. A century. I'd be dead by then. But what about our kids? I assumed he'd look after any who were demons once I was gone. That is, if we ever decided to have children. After raising my six siblings, I wasn't sure I wanted to go down that path again.

"A century." He reached out and cupped my chin. "There's a place in hell for you, if this works out between us."

I couldn't help laughing. "Oh gee thanks! I'm so glad to know I'll be welcome in hell. And you do realize that in a century I'll be dead."

He chuckled. "Yes, well since all the humans in hell are dead, you'll fit right in. I know of a few witches there, so you won't be missing out on intellectual conversation of the spell casting type."

"You're proposing that I go to hell?" It would have been funny if it wasn't so alarming.

"Well, yeah. Eventually I'm hoping you will. It doesn't have to be forever. I mean, my mother finally got fed up with my father after a few thousand years and ditched hell."

"I'll be dead, and I get the feeling I won't be welcome in heaven if I've been down in hell with a demon lover." Come to think of it, I'm not sure I wasn't damning myself just sleeping with him while I was alive. What were the theological implications of this relationship?

"Cassie, it's not like that. Hell isn't all brimstone and fire and torture."

"Lava pit spa treatment?" I grinned. "Chocolate? Pizza? How's the shopping?"

"Well, no shopping. But you could always vacation here and hit the outlets if you feel the need."

This didn't sound much like hell. "I'll be dead, a spirit. What good would shopping do me as a ghost let out of hell for a weekend getaway?"

"A ghost? No, sweetheart. You're not understanding this. You're not going to be some damned soul. There are…there are benefits to being the lover of a demon. And there are special benefits to being the lover of the son of Satan. Not tooting my own horn here, it's just the way it is. You'll gain in power. Over time, you'll be my equal."

"And why didn't you lead with these perks when you were trying to seduce me?" I teased.

"Because it took all of five minutes to seduce you and there wasn't much talking involved?"

I whacked him with the spoon and he laughed.

"Actually, as a witch I thought you knew these things." He grinned. "One night with me does confer some benefits, but a long-time relationship? Us in love? You'd be a high-level demon after your death. And alive you'll find your powers increasing year by year."

I set down the spoon and stepped into him. "It's not the perks, buddy. I want to know that I won't be trapped in hell, tortured for all eternity because you got pissed off at me or decided you didn't want me anymore."

He laughed. "You're a witch, Cassie. You with your coven of sisters are more than capable of holding your own against me. And by the time you're in hell…well, I'm probably the one who should be worried you'd decide to ditch me and dump me in a lava pit."

"Well then keep that in mind if you ever think of screwing around." I gave him a quick kiss, then handed him the bowl of green beans. "Now let's go eat. Everything else is on the table and our family is out there starving."

He leaned down and kissed me, slow and soft and full of promise. "As you command, my witch. As you command."

ACKNOWLEDGMENTS

Thanks to my copyeditor Jennifer Cosham whose eagle eyes catch all the typos and keep my comma problem in line, and to Renee George for cover design.

ABOUT THE AUTHOR

Debra lives in a little house in the woods of Maryland with her sons and two slobbery bloodhounds. On a good day, she jogs and horseback rides, hopefully managing to keep the horse between herself and the ground. Her only known super power is 'Identify Roadkill'.

For more information:
www.debradunbar.com
Debra Dunbar's Author page

ALSO BY DEBRA DUNBAR

Accidental Witches Series

Brimstone and Broomsticks

Warmongers and Wands (Feb 2019)

Death and Divination (March 2019)

White Lightning Series

Wooden Nickels

Bum's Rush

Clip Joint

Jake Walk

Trouble Boys (2019)

***

The Templar Series

Dead Rising

Last Breath

Bare Bones

Famine's Feast

Royal Blood (2019)

Dark Crossroads (2019)

* * *

IMP WORLD NOVELS

The Imp Series

A Demon Bound

Satan's Sword

Elven Blood

Devil's Paw

Imp Forsaken

Angel of Chaos

Kingdom of Lies

Exodus

Queen of the Damned

The Morning Star

* * *

<u>Half-breed Series</u>

Demons of Desire

Sins of the Flesh

Cornucopia

Unholy Pleasures

City of Lust

* * *

<u>Imp World Novels</u>

No Man's Land

Stolen Souls

Three Wishes

Northern Lights

Far From Center

Penance

* * *

<u>Northern Wolves</u>

Juneau to Kenai

Rogue

Winter Fae

Bad Seed

www.ingramcontent.com/pod-product-compliance
Lightning Source LLC
Chambersburg PA
CBHW050534190726

48284CB00003B/1067